"Where are th[e]
fleet officers?[]

The Orion leader, Chogu, sat down in the captain's chair and thumped his dirty booted feet up on the desktop.

He doesn't know! That means they're still free! "Sorry, I can't help you," Deanna answered pleasantly.

The subordinate Orion aimed his disruptor at Deanna as Chogu grinned. "Let us exchange favors, Starfleet ensign." He held up her commbadge. "Contact your people. Find out where they are hiding. In return, I will let you live."

Deanna's response came with surprising ease. She said nothing.

"I am waiting," Chogu prompted.

Deanna just looked at him.

Chogu nodded, as if he respected her courage. "Do not fear. I will allow you to live . . . for now." He motioned for his subordinate to follow him out of the office. The door locked behind them.

Deanna sat down on the deck, trying to get as comfortable as she could with her hands tied behind her back. "Good job, Ensign Troi," she grumbled to herself. "How long did it take you to get caught—maybe five minutes?"

STAR TREK
THE NEXT GENERATION®

STARFLEET ACADEMY® #12
BREAKAWAY

Bobbi JG Weiss and
David Cody Weiss

**Interior Illustrations by
Todd Cameron Hamilton**

A
MINSTREL®
BOOK

Published by POCKET BOOKS
New York   London   Toronto   Sydney   Tokyo   Singapore

A MINSTREL PAPERBACK *Original*

 A Minstrel Book published by
POCKET BOOKS, a division of Simon & Schuster Inc.
1230 Avenue of the Americas, New York, NY 10020

STAR TREK is a Registered Trademark of Paramount Pictures.

A VIACOM COMPANY

This book is published by Pocket Books, a division of Simon & Schuster Inc., under exclusive license from Paramount Pictures.

ISBN: 0-671-00226-0

First Minstrel Books printing April 1997

10 9 8 7 6 5 4 3 2 1

A MINSTREL BOOK and colophon are registered trademarks of Simon & Schuster Inc.

Cover art by Donato Giancola

Printed in the U.S.A.

For Carl and Marge—we done it!

STARFLEET TIMELINE

2264

The launch of Captain James T. Kirk's five-year mission, _U.S.S. Enterprise,_ NCC-1701.

2292

Alliance between the Klingon Empire and the Romulan Star Empire collapses.

2293

Colonel Worf, grandfather of Worf Rozhenko, defends Captain Kirk and Doctor McCoy at their trial for the murder of Klingon chancellor Gorkon.

Khitomer Peace Conference, Klingon Empire/Federation (_Star Trek VI_).

2323

Jean-Luc Picard enters Starfleet Academy's standard four-year program.

2328

The Cardassian Empire annexes the Bajoran homeworld.

2341

Data enters Starfleet Academy.

2342

Beverly Crusher (née Howard) enters Starfleet Academy Medical School, an eight-year program.

2346

Romulan massacre of Klingon outpost on Khitomer.

2351

In orbit around Bajor, the Cardassians construct a space station
that they will later abandon.

2353

William T. Riker and Geordi La Forge enter Starfleet Academy.

2354

Deanna Troi enters Starfleet Academy.

2356

Tasha Yar enters Starfleet Academy.

2357

Worf Rozhenko enters Starfleet Academy.

2363

Captain Jean-Luc Picard assumes command of U.S.S. Enterprise, NCC-1701-D.

2367

Wesley Crusher enters Starfleet Academy.

An uneasy truce is signed between the Cardassians and the Federation.

Borg attack at Wolf 359; First Officer Lieutenant Commander
Benjamin Sisko and his son, Jake, are among the survivors.

U.S.S. Enterprise-D defeats the Borg vessel in orbit around Earth.

2369

Commander Benjamin Sisko assumes command of Deep Space
Nine in orbit over Bajor.

Source: Star Trek® Chronology / Michael Okuda and Denise Okuda

BREAKAWAY

CHAPTER

1

Cargo Freighter
Alpha Quadrant, Sector C

Ensign Deanna Troi ran full tilt down the ship's corridor, banging her shoulder against the bulkhead as she careened around a corner. Pain shot down her arm, but she ignored it. She'd have to deal with far worse if her pursuers captured her.

They're right behind you! she thought frantically as the bulkheads whizzed past. Another corner loomed ahead. She skidded around it—

Dead end!

Deanna quickly looked around, spotted an access hatch in the deck several meters away, and yanked it up. The service ladder below led down to the freighter's cargo holds. Hiding among the cargo might be her only chance.

Deanna swung herself onto the ladder and closed the hatch over her head, locking it shut just as the pounding footfalls of her pursuers drew near. "Take that!" she muttered, melting the locking mechanism with a short phaser blast. "Let's see if you can catch me now!"

As she scrambled down the ladder, Deanna's mind raced. *Those Orion pirates came out of nowhere! One minute we were alone on the bridge, and the next minute they were materializing right in front of us!* The odds were in the Orions' favor from the start—six of them against five Starfleet officers, and the attackers had the element of surprise. Deanna and her away team hadn't even had time to draw their phasers before they were forced to scatter under a barrage of deadly disruptor fire. The Orions had taken up the chase with fierce delight.

Deanna picked a deck at random, jumped off the ladder, and started running again. She slapped her commbadge, hoping for a reply but not really expecting one. Twice before, the device had produced nothing but static, and she got nothing but static now. *The Orions must be jamming our frequencies,* she thought as she ran. Then how would she ever rejoin her comrades? *Don't worry, you'll find them,* she promised herself. *They're probably hiding. Find a safe place to catch your breath, then use your empathic abilities to search them out.*

At this moment Deanna's empathic abilities were of little help. She couldn't contact her people, couldn't see them, couldn't hear them. All she could sense was their fear mixed with hard determination as they raced through the mazelike corridors of the old cargo freighter, just as she was doing. None of them were hurt, but Deanna dreaded the moment when she might empathically feel that status change. Somehow the away team had to regroup, but how? Where? *Find them,* she kept repeating as she ran. *You've got to find them!* She rounded another corner—

"N'dabe kuhg!" shouted a harsh, deep voice.

Reflexes responded faster than thought. In a flash Deanna's phaser was in her hand and she was blasting away at two Orions standing not ten meters in front of her. Their sudden appearance startled her enough that her shots went wild, but those shots were enough to drive the enemy back and around a corner. She sprinted down a long straightaway, praying she'd reach the end of it before the Orions resumed their chase.

No such luck. Though the Orions were still far behind, one of them managed to get off a disruptor shot that sizzled past Deanna's head so close that the heat of it made her wince. The blast hit an emergency equipment locker, and she was thrown against the bulkhead as the cabinet exploded. Her body lurched through space, an odd slow-motion sensation that felt

as if she were somehow floating upward and hitting her head on the ceiling.

But when everything stopped spinning, Deanna found herself lying on the deck. Her head pounded with pain, and a loud buzzing sound reverberated in her skull. *What hit me?* came the fuzzy thought. Then her bleary eyes fixed on a small emergency oxygen canister lying nearby. *It must have hit my head when the cabinet exploded.*

Smoke billowed through the air, but Deanna resisted the temptation to cough. The Orions were still far away. If they believed she was dead, they'd take their time coming. Her only chance was to escape before the smoke cleared.

Slowly she rose to her hands and knees. *Your phaser! You dropped it when you fell!* Quickly Deanna felt around the floor for it, but she touched only the scattered contents of the emergency locker. *You're running out of time! They'll be here any second!*

Then something caught her eye—a service closet! Even through the smoke she could make out its dark square shape.

Deanna scrambled inside, barely managing to slap the CLOSE touchpad control before the sound of booted feet approached at a slow, confident trot. The footsteps stopped. Metal clanked against metal—one of the Orions must have kicked the oxygen canister with his metal-toed boot—and a gruff voice spoke. Even though Deanna didn't know his language, the pirate's curt tone clearly indicated anger. Snarling, he and his partner sped to the end of the straightaway, paused, then continued down the next corridor, their pounding footsteps fading away until the only sound Deanna could hear was the buzzing in her own head.

You're safe, she thought with relief. The closet door must have sealed so seamlessly it was invisible in all the smoke outside. As far as the pirates knew, Deanna had simply disappeared.

With a trembling hand she brushed a strand of hair out of her eyes. The gash on her forehead throbbed, and the buzzing in her head was growing louder by the minute, as if her pain had taken on a life of its own. She gasped and, leaning back against the bulkhead, tried to relax. *You might be in here a long time. Get some rest while you can.*

Fatigue suddenly took her. Her eyelids drooped. Her strength failed. As Deanna Troi collapsed to the floor, a question floated up through the muzziness of her brain. *How did you get yourself into this mess, Deanna? How in the world did you get into this mess?*

CHAPTER

2

Starfleet Academy
Earth

Buzzing. There was a loud buzzing noise in her head, as if a thousand angry bees were swarming inside her skull.

Cadet Deanna Troi shook her head to clear it, but she succeeded only in making herself dizzy. A strong, cool hand steadied her. "Need you support?" inquired a pleasant gurgly voice.

It was the Ichthyan female. Deanna remembered seeing her in the shuttle, sitting alone in the back, a tall regal figure with iridescent blue-green scales instead of skin and a tumble of long, thick red-brown hair framing

7

her exotic features. Except for the fact that she had two human-shaped legs instead of one long fin, she might have been a fairy-tale mermaid princess. She was stunning.

Deanna smiled up at her. "Thank you, I'm fine now."

The Ichthyan inclined her head politely, then turned back to what they'd both been doing—staring at the grounds of Starfleet Academy spread out before them like a beckoning dream.

But this is no dream, Deanna thought, glancing back at the shuttle that had just deposited her and the other new cadets on the Academy's landing field. *I'm here. I'm finally here!*

A career in Starfleet—adventure, exploration, the chance to work with people from the hundreds of worlds within the Federation—it was everything Deanna could ever wish for. But even better than that, it was a chance to be on her own. From now on, Deanna could run her life the way she wanted to. Finally she could rely on her own judgment, make her own choices, lead her own—

She winced again as her head throbbed with pain. The Ichthyan leaned over and peered into her face with concern. "You are not well."

"I'm fine!" Deanna snapped. The harshness of her own voice startled her. "I mean . . . please forgive me. I really am okay. I just have to adjust to being on a planet where people don't shield their emotions. You see, I'm an empath."

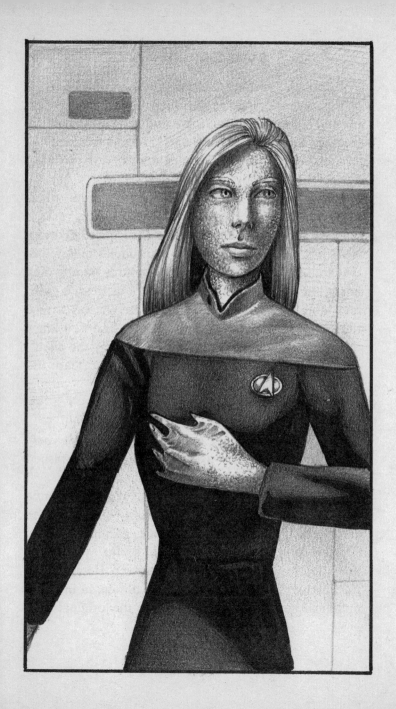

"Em-path?" repeated the Ichthyan curiously.

"I can sense other people's emotions," Deanna explained. "Most Betazoids are full telepaths, and we learn to shield our feelings and thoughts from others. Terrans don't shield their emotions." She winced again. "In fact, they're quite loud."

The Ichthyan's sea-blue eyes grew wide. "This pains you?"

"Yes, a little." Then Deanna shrugged. "Okay, a lot. I just have to build up my own shields in defense, that's all." Through the riot of emotions bombarding her brain, Deanna felt the Ichthyan's distress, a clear, high note of concern for her welfare. It was a nice thing to feel in this strange new place. "Look, I knew this would happen," she added, touched by the alien's concern. "It's one of the things I'll have to learn if I expect to become a Starfleet officer."

The Ichthyan nodded in understanding. "Yes, we all have many new things to learn."

And not all of them have to do with classwork, Deanna thought. A wave of homesickness washed over her, and she sighed.

What was Lwaxana Troi doing right now? Deanna figured that her mother was probably sitting on the garden porch feeling terribly alone, gazing up at the sky and thinking of her only child so far away. Even now, across all the light-years between Betazed and Earth, Deanna could feel Lwaxana tug on an invisible umbilical cord, a cord that, unlike the original one, still held mother and daughter very close. But now the tug of that cord hurt. It felt like guilt.

Don't think that way! Deanna sternly thought to herself. *It's time to cut that cord once and for all. Mother was smothering you. She didn't give you a moment to yourself. You've got to live your own life!*

Still the guilt pulled at her, deep inside. Deanna made herself recall the argument that had almost kept her from applying to the Academy. "What in Nine Fires has gotten into you, Little One?" Lwaxana had said, flinging her arms in the air with typical hyperdramatic emphasis. "You're from a noble family, and you want to run off and join an organization where you'll be duty-bound to obey the orders of any pipsqueak who happens to have more of those little silver dot-things on his uniform collar than you do. What kind of life is that for an heir to the Holy Rings of Betazed?"

Deanna suspected that her mother was trying to irritate her into giving up. Lwaxana knew full well what those "little silver dot-things" were. They were called pips, and they denoted a Starfleet officer's rank. "I want to have a chance to earn my own rank," Deanna said. "If I stay here on Betazed, my whole life will be planned for me." She hoped her mother didn't mind such a blatant accusation. After all, it was Lwaxana who would do all the planning if Deanna stayed. "I want to see what I can do by myself, Mother. Can't you understand that?"

But all Lwaxana could see was her noble daughter taking orders from pipsqueaks with lots of "little dot-things" on their collars. After an hour's grueling argument, however, Lwaxana gave in. "Oh, all right, all right, all right! You may take the entrance exams. But," she added, "only if you apply for the command track."

"*What?* Mother, I don't want to command other people!" Deanna protested.

Lwaxana shrugged. "I'm sorry, Deanna, but I will not see my daughter waste precious years pooping decks on starships out in the middle of some black hole just to earn enough dots to get the respect she deserves by plain and simple breeding. You should be giving orders, not taking them. No," she said with finality, "it's the command track or nothing."

So Deanna was in the command track. Amazingly, she'd scored well enough on her entrance exam to merit the position. But if she failed now . . . oh, boy, she'd never hear the end of it.

The Ichthyan's gurgly voice broke through Deanna's brooding. "I wish you success in all your endeavors, fellow cadet." And with that, the alien picked up her bag and followed the other cadets who had debarked the shuttle and were now on their way to the administration building to check in.

Deanna looked around. She was the only one still on the landing pad. The shuttle captain eyed her, tapping his foot impatiently. "Oh—sorry," Deanna muttered. She picked up her bag and hurried after the other cadets, hoping she had the strength to face the challenges ahead.

*   *   *

The next two weeks flew by in a blur of new experiences—new classes, new faces, new routines, even a crisp new cadet's uniform. A fast-paced excitement pervaded Starfleet Academy, as if the air itself were charged with the energy of learning. Deanna should have been having the time of her life.

But she wasn't.

Strengthening her mental shields turned out to be more difficult than she'd expected. No matter how hard she concentrated, there were times when she felt as if her own thoughts and emotions were getting smashed into a tiny corner of her skull while the emotions of every other sentient being within ten kilometers crammed in to use up all available thinking room. She couldn't concentrate. She was irritable and snappish. Regular relaxation periods and plenty of sleep might have helped, but Deanna could hardly manage either of those things under the pressure of her class load.

She didn't dare tell anyone. Who would sympathize? After all, Deanna wasn't the first empath to attend the Academy. If she let on that she was having problems, they might think her unfit for Starfleet. "Building proper mental shields is a skill, Little One," Lwaxana had warned her before she left home. "Living on Betazed all your life, why, you're used to dealing with highly disciplined telepaths who'd never dream of letting their emotions fly helter-skelter. But on Earth it's quite another thing. You really ought to wait until you master more techniques."

Deanna had been sure that her mother was just trying to keep her from leaving home. Now she realized that Lwaxana was right. But right or not, Deanna would manage. She had to.

At least her living arrangements turned out well. Her assigned roommate was Twil d-ch-Ka, the Ichthyan she'd met on the day of her arrival. "Twil. That's a pretty name," Deanna told her.

"Twil designates clan, and d-ch-Ka designates my person." The Ichthyan put a bizarre accent on the name that Deanna couldn't even hope to duplicate. "The meaning is 'fire beneath the waves.'"

Fire indeed, Deanna noted. D-ch-Ka's long red hair was in striking contrast to her cool ocean-colored body.

Ichthos was a water world, and though the Ichthyans dwelled in great cities that floated above the waves, they spent most of their time wet. D-ch-Ka was every inch a swimmer, from her webbed fingers and toes to the natural racing lines of her sleek humanoid body. Her scales were soft, and they glittered in the light. The lotion that d-ch-Ka used to maintain sufficient body moisture added to the effect, making her glisten with an almost magical effect in full sunlight.

Deanna liked her from the start. But she couldn't pronounce her name correctly no matter how hard she tried. "Tell you what," Deanna offered. "Suppose I call you by a nickname instead?"

"Nickname? That is a term of belonging, correct?"

D-ch-Ka's eyes sparkled with pleasure. "Yes, you will designate for me a nickname!"

Deanna couldn't help but laugh at the delight radiating from the normally aristocratic Ichthyan. "Okay," she said thoughtfully, "how about, umm . . . Auburn?"

D-ch-Ka just stared, clueless.

"Auburn is a shade of red," Deanna explained. "The color of your hair."

Now d-ch-Ka grinned. "I approve!"

The nickname caught on, and soon every cadet who met the tall Ichthyan knew her as Auburn. She was becoming quite popular.

Strangely enough, Deanna herself wasn't doing so well in that area. In fact, for the first time in her life, Deanna Troi was having trouble making friends. Auburn seemed to be the only person whose emotions didn't cause Deanna mental distress. The Ichthyan's mind was calm and cool, like a tranquil ocean. Her emotions brushed up against Deanna's mental shields like soft waves lapping at a beach, not like a pack of frenzied Klingon targs trying to tear down a wall. Deanna didn't know if all Ichthyans enjoyed such a peaceful mental state, but one thing was clear—almost every other life-form at the Academy, particularly humans, did not.

"I don't understand it," Deanna told Auburn during their second week at the Academy. "I've never had trouble being sociable before."

They were walking into the mess hall for dinner, and the big room was fluttering with activity, lots of chatting and slurping, scraping chairs and clanking silverware. It sounded nothing like the orderly, servant-filled Troi household on Betazed, but Deanna presumed it reminded other cadets of home sweet home.

"I've met a lot of people here," Deanna continued as she and Auburn headed for the counter laden with the evening's food choices, "but I don't seem to be making a good impression."

Auburn said nothing as the two of them scanned the available plates on the counter. Then suddenly Deanna gasped. "I don't believe it!"

"Excuse?" Auburn asked.

Deanna snatched a little glass bowl of rich brown foam off the counter, her mouth watering. "Unless I'm mistaken, this is Thalian chocolate mousse. Thalian chocolate is the richest chocolate in the galaxy!"

"Hey, you can't take dessert yet," said a short, studious cadet behind her. His name was Ned Kenrick, and he lived three doors down the hall from Deanna and Auburn. "You haven't eaten a main course. You'd better put it back."

A sensation of paranoia shot out from Ned and pierced Deanna's mental shields, smothering her good mood like a wet blanket on a fire. "What's the matter with you, Kenrick?" she barked at the cadet. "Are you so paranoid that you actually think they're watching to see if we eat our meals in order?" And with that she pushed her way out of the line and began looking for an unoccupied table, the bowl of mousse cupped protectively in her hands.

What's the matter with you? Deanna angrily asked herself. *You're acting like a child. Now everybody's staring.* Indeed, she felt as if every pair of eyes in the mess hall was following her every move.

In truth, only a few cadets had witnessed the outburst. But Deanna felt as if everyone was now judging her on the great cosmic scale of worthiness. *It's not fair!* she thought, plunking herself down at a corner table, away from everyone else. *Every time I think my shields are firmly in place, somebody comes along and throws his mental static right at me. Then people act as if* I've *done something wrong. They don't understand what I'm going through!*

Deanna grabbed up her spoon and started eating. The foam was Thalian chocolate mousse, all right. Its creamy smoothness calmed her down. *If only life could be as smooth as chocolate,* she thought dismally, scooping up another spoonful, then another.

Then she stopped, wondering. Maybe Ned was right. Maybe someone *was* watching the cadets all the time, even here, monitoring their actions and choices, making little notes that went into their permanent files, recording every single—

No! she thought angrily. *Deanna, that's not how you feel. That's how* Ned *feels. His paranoia is still in your head. Get it* out!

She suddenly looked up to find Auburn seated across the table from her, gazing at her over a plate of raw seafood. As she'd done with her mother so many times, Deanna wiped the expression of rage from her face and instantly replaced it with one of innocent calm. "Is something wrong?" she inquired.

"I am wondering that of you," Auburn gurgled, and pointed at Deanna's bowl with a long blue finger.

The bowl was empty. Deanna blinked down at it in surprise. "It was . . . really good," was all she could think of to say.

Auburn plucked a bite-sized octopus from her plate and popped it into her mouth. "Before the Thalian chocolate, you expressed to me a concern," she said after swallowing the little sea creature whole.

Deanna didn't follow.

"A concern about impressions you fail to make on others?" Auburn prompted.

Out of nowhere, the image of Lwaxana flooded Deanna's mind. "First impressions are everything, Little One," her mother had once told her. "Why, just look at me, for instance. I always dress in my very best, and my manners are impeccable. After all, you never know who you may have to impress!"

"Be quiet, Mother," Deanna said quietly through clenched teeth.

Auburn leaned forward, as if trying to hear a whisper. "Repeat, please?"

"Oh, uh . . . I was just thinking." Deanna toyed with her spoon, wishing she had more chocolate mousse. "Auburn, by now everyone knows I'm an empath. Why can't they at least *try* to understand what I'm going through? They treat me like an ogre or something."

The Ichthyan smiled gently. "The truth of Deanna

Troi is buried deep, but I believe I see it." She leaned forward. "Do you wish to hear truth?"

Deanna shivered a little. "If it will help me . . . yes."

Auburn spoke mildly but to the point. "You led a privileged life on Betazed, Troi. For this reason you carry yourself in a haughty manner. Others are afraid to approach, though they may wish to."

Deanna started to defend herself, then clamped her lips shut and just listened.

"You possess impressive beauty in the eyes of many cultures," Auburn continued in a matter-of-fact tone, adding, "Ichthyans included. Such beauty intimidates others."

Beauty? Intimidating? Deanna wondered at that, but held her tongue.

"Your empathic gifts still pain you," Auburn went on. "You struggle to shield yourself from the emotions of others, but your efforts give your face an appearance of"—Auburn paused, and Deanna held her breath—"anger. None wish to meet an angry person."

"I'm not always angry!" Deanna finally blurted out. "I'm just having trouble keeping my shields strong. It takes a lot of concentration." For someone like Lwaxana, it would be a snap. But Deanna was new at this. She was trying so hard! Couldn't the other cadets see that?

"I also note," Auburn said dryly, "that you often contradict others."

"I do not—" Deanna stopped. *Oh, good grief . . .*

"Perhaps," Auburn suggested calmly, "it is a strong

desire to be independent that makes you reject the suggestions of others, even those suggestions concerning noncritical subjects."

Deanna cringed. "Like when to eat dessert." She wanted to crawl under a rock. "I see now, Auburn. Thank you." *No wonder nobody wants to talk to me! How could I have been so blind?* Swallowing her pride, Deanna drew herself up straight again and met Auburn's gaze. "All right, so . . . what can I do?"

The Ichthyan pondered a moment. "You are complex, Troi. This is not one problem, but many. I offer you the advice my father offered me before I left Ichthos: 'See all, but act only on truth.' "

Deanna nodded. She knew good advice when she heard it.

Deanna maneuvered her way down the crowded corridor of the xenosciences building, clutching her computer padd close as if it might shield her from the riot of emotions whirling around her head, trying to get in. She was not happy. Things just weren't working out.

All the truth that Auburn had given her a week ago in the mess hall, all that stuff about being haughty and unapproachable and angry—it had sounded correctable at the time. But Deanna had spent this whole week trying to change her ways, and things were only getting worse.

For instance, she should have been happy right now. She had just gotten a perfect score on a Basic Navigation pop quiz, and navigation theory wasn't even her specialty. But she'd studied the instructor, Lieutenant Takota, as much as she had the class material. One thing had been obvious to her from day one: Takota was a man who liked surprises. It was only natural to expect him to throw surprises at his students. When he popped the quiz, she was ready.

Alex Renny, a Basic Nav classmate, hadn't been ready at all. When the test scores were announced, his envy had overwhelmed her mental shields and polluted her thoughts, giving her a headache worse than any she'd had since arriving at the Academy.

As Deanna bulldozed her way through the crowd, heading for the xenosociology lecture hall, she sensed an uncomfortable presence close behind her. Too close. She whirled around and, sure enough, there stood Alex Renny.

Renny put his hands up as if to ward off a wild beast. "Hey!" he cried defensively.

Deanna realized that she was the beast. Her expression was set in a furious frown, her eyes narrowed. "Hey what?" she asked back, trying to keep the challenge out of her voice and failing.

Renny lowered his hands. "I just wanted to congratulate you, Cadet Troi. You did, after all, score a perfect one hundred on a killer quiz."

"I study a lot," Deanna answered carefully, sensing the hot, unpleasant wave of negativity emanating from him. She did her best to keep her shields strong. "Excuse me, I have to get to class."

But Renny followed her. "You're Betazoid, right?"

Deanna stopped. "Yes, I am. Well, half Betazoid. My father was human."

"So you can read minds?"

"No, I'm an empath. I can read emotions but not thoughts."

Renny shook his head sympathetically. "Too bad. Mind reading would sure come in handy at test time, I bet."

Deanna froze. *So that's what this is all about,* she thought. "I did not cheat on that pop quiz, Mr. Renny," she told him flatly.

With puppy-innocent eyes, Renny held up his hands again. "Whoa, now, I never said you did."

"But you feel that way."

"Ah, so you *can* read minds!"

"It doesn't take telepathy to tell you're angry at me for scoring better than you," Deanna retorted. "That's not fair."

"Funny you should use that word—'fair,' " Renny said, his voice low. "What's not fair is that a mind reader can take an exam in a classroom full of non-telepaths."

"I told you—"

"You told me you were *empathic,* okay," Renny corrected himself. "But that still means you can sense things in other people's minds. There's no normal way you could have scored one hundred on that test. Admit it."

Deanna pulled herself up to full height, a move she'd seen her mother make when preparing to answer a direct challenge. With an aristocratic air that sounded more like Lwaxana than she cared to admit, Deanna said, "Just because I knew that Lieutenant Takota would give us a pop quiz—"

Renny's eyes widened. "You knew?"

Oops! Deanna winced at her own poor choice of words. "I mean . . . I expected one. Takota's the type to give pop quizzes, that's obvious."

Renny's expression indicated that it had not been obvious to him.

"Look," Deanna said, "I really do have to get to my next class." She made a hasty retreat, thinking, *Shields, Deanna! Block his emotions. Don't let him get to you.*

But Renny wasn't finished. "Deanna, wait!" He caught up with her, stepped in her path, and forced her to stop. "Just look at it from my point of view—"

"It seems to me, Mr. Renny, that your point of view focuses on excuses, not performance," Deanna said frostily. "I may not be a quantum mechanics major, but that doesn't mean I'm stupid."

"But you're rich," Renny countered. "They say you got special tutoring just to get into the Academy. And I looked you up—your father was in Starfleet and your mother has Federation connections. Look, all I'm trying to say is, you have an advantage and it's not fair. How can I hope to compete with you?"

"You're not supposed to compete with me," Deanna said, forcing her voice to remain calm as she backed away. "Now please leave me alone." She

whirled around and headed for the double doors leading to the xenosociology lecture hall.

"You just can't see it from my point of view, can
you?" Renny called after her. "Hey, I had to work
my rear off to get here, while you—"

Deanna finally exploded. She whipped around and
faced Renny for what she hoped would be the last
time. "I am not a cheater! I do not read minds to get
good grades. I gained admittance to Starfleet Academy because I deserved it, and neither my father nor
my mother had anything whatsoever to do with it."
And with that, Deanna banged through the door leading to the lecture hall.

And saw Lwaxana Troi standing on the dais, smiling
at her.

Deanna's jaw dropped, and so did the padd in her
hand.

CHAPTER

3

Cargo Freighter
Alpha Quadrant, Sector C

Deanna's jaw dropped in surprise as the door of the service closet *whooshed* open. Bright light from the corridor spilled into her dark little sanctuary, and she recoiled from the glare, groping blindly for a weapon. Her fingers curled around the handle of a heavy anti-grav wand, and despite her momentary blindness she lunged out into the corridor, swinging.

Something very strong jerked the wand out of her grasp. "N'ghu ke!" an Orion shouted.

Deanna's arms were wrenched behind her back, and her wrists were tied with what felt like leather thongs.

26

She winced but made no sound as the Orion who'd spoken, clearly the leader of the pirates, slowly circled her. She made out more of his features and clothing as her eyes adjusted to the bright light of the corridor.

The humanoid Orions weren't tall, nor were they particularly massive. But there was a sense of solidity about them which suggested that nothing short of a Brikarian wrestler could push them off-balance. They all wore similar clothing—pants and vests of a thick leatherlike material, cut and arranged like armor plating, and heavy boots. Their black hair was long and tangled, their skin was green, and they apparently didn't value personal hygiene. Deanna almost gagged as the Orion pirate captain leaned close and rasped, "Starfleet ensign. I am Captain Chogu."

Should she respond? Deanna knew that Orions had little respect for females of their own species, let alone females who held positions of importance in other cultures. Keeping quiet might be a wise choice.

Chogu grabbed her arm just roughly enough to emphasize who was in charge. "Boduk ru ma!" he shouted.

"Chogu!" she responded hastily.

He let go of her, apparently satisfied with the response. "You note, I think, that your communications device"—he gestured at her commbadge—"does not function. We have blanketed this ship with an interference field. You will not contact your people."

He motioned at his two subordinates. One of them

raised a disruptor to cover Deanna while the other seized her commbadge and tricorder.

"We found your phaser," Chogu informed her. "And this I will keep, just in case." He grabbed her commbadge from his subordinate and tucked it into a pocket. Then he gestured again, and Deanna was pushed forward.

The Orions marched her through the ship. The freighter appeared to be deserted, but Deanna knew better. The ship's crew, her away team members, and the other three Orions were on board somewhere. She hoped her comrades were still free.

They arrived at the captain's office. Chogu sat down in the captain's chair and thumped his dirty booted feet up on the desktop. "Where are the other Starfleet officers?" he asked with mild menace.

He doesn't know! That means they're still free! "Sorry, I can't help you," Deanna answered pleasantly.

The subordinate Orion aimed his disruptor at Deanna as Chogu grinned, displaying a rather nauseating set of broken yellow teeth. "Let us exchange favors, Starfleet ensign." He held up her commbadge. "Contact your people. Find out where they are hiding. In return, I will let you live."

Deanna's response came with surprising ease. She said nothing.

"I am waiting," Chogu prompted.

Deanna just looked at him.

Chogu nodded, and the subordinate Orion kicked

Deanna's legs out from under her. She collapsed to her knees so fast she didn't even have time to cry out in surprise or pain. "Do not fear," Chogu told her gently, rising from his chair. "I will allow you to live." As he and his subordinate walked out of the office he added, "You will bring a fine price at the slave market."

The second they were gone, Deanna cleared her mind and then slowly, carefully lowered her mental shields. Yes, there they were, all four of her away team members. She could sense their fear, some excitement, even a feeling of triumph from one. But she still had no idea where they were or whether she would ever see them again.

Deanna sat down on the deck, trying to get as comfortable as she could with her hands tied behind her back. "Good job, Ensign Troi," she grumbled to herself. "How long did it take you to get caught—maybe five minutes?" She looked around, trying to ignore the painful throbbing in her head and knees.

The pirates must have cleaned the captain's cabin out before bringing her here. There was very little in it, just the desk and chair, a bare table, and a matching armoire and trunk, all locked and bolted to the floor. Deanna could see nothing from which she might make a tool or weapon.

She slumped in despair. *It's not supposed to turn out like this. I've hardly had a chance, and it's all over.* Starfleet meant so much to her, and she'd worked so hard. . . .

No, Deanna, don't give in to despair! If you can't find a way to escape, then just rest and wait. Let them give you an opening if you can't make one yourself.

Good advice. Deanna was surprised that she'd given it to herself. *All right, then,* she answered her own mental voice, *I'll wait, save my energy, and let the Orions call the shots.*

Deanna found herself mulling over the events that had brought her to this awful situation. It had started so simply. Her ship, the *U.S.S. Chippewa,* had intercepted an automated distress call from the Alpha Centurian freighter *Borocco-Kai.* Deanna was assigned to the away team that was to beam over and investigate.

The away team beamed directly to the *Borocco-Kai*'s bridge, only to find the bridge crew dead. Just as they called in to report, an Orion pirate ship, hidden by a Romulan cloaking device, suddenly appeared and attacked the *Chippewa.* Captain Tallerday was forced to raise the *Chippewa*'s shields, leaving Deanna's away team to secure the freighter and, if possible, rescue the civilian crew.

But six Orions had then beamed onto the freighter's bridge and immediately opened fire. The away team had scattered, Deanna had been cut off from the others, and now she was caught like a rabbit in a trap.

CHAPTER

4

Starfleet Academy
Earth

It was like being caught in a trap. Without warning, Deanna found herself standing in the doorway of the xenosociology lecture hall, staring in mute shock at her mother up on the lecture stage!

Surprise! came Lwaxana's mental voice. *I shielded my thoughts from you so you'd never suspect I was here.* Lwaxana suddenly frowned and gestured down at Deanna's feet. *Pick up your padd, dear, before someone trips over it.*

Like a robot, Deanna bent down, picked up her data padd, then straightened up. Her arms twitched slightly as if she suffered from a nervous tic. By now the other students were watching her, wondering if she was having some sort of seizure. *Mother*— Deanna finally projected, but that was as far as she got.

I know, I know. What in the name of Nine Fires am I doing here? Lwaxana interrupted, and then laughed out loud.

Now all the cadets in the room turned their attention from Deanna to Lwaxana. Deanna sensed their collective responses shift from confusion to understanding as they realized they were witnessing two Betazoids having a telepathic conversation. *So what are you doing here, Mother?* Deanna finally demanded.

Why, I'm the guest lecturer, Lwaxana replied cheerily. She pointed at an empty chair directly in front of the dais. *Now hurry up and sit down so I can start. I saved this seat just for you.*

Deanna was too flabbergasted to do anything but follow Lwaxana's pointing finger and sit down. *Mother, I'm having enough trouble as it is,* she cried, *and now this! You never told me. . . . You never considered what this might do to me!*

By now the room was filled with cadets, and they were all staring at Deanna and her mother. Lwaxana turned to them and opened her arms as if to embrace them one and all, but she directed her thoughts to Deanna. *I know perfectly well what my presence will do for you, Little One, but let's talk about that later. Right now I have a lecture to give. Take notes!*

"Greetings, cadets!" Lwaxana said aloud, cranking

her radiant smile up full blast. "I am Lwaxana Troi of Betazed, daughter of the Fifth House, Holder of the Sacred Chalice of Rixx, and Heir to the Holy Rings of Betazed. And this," she added, "is my lovely daughter, Deanna." Lwaxana gestured to Deanna as if she were introducing royalty.

Deanna gasped and ducked down as far as she could without crawling under her chair. *No, Mother, don't, please!*

Hush, dear, Mother's teaching. "Now, this may be only your third xenosociology class," Lwaxana said, "but there's already been a change in the, uh . . . oh, for heaven's sake, what's it called again? The syllabus! Yes, that's it. Your excellent instructor, Mr. Mathias, has decided to split his lecture duties this semester with me."

Deanna wanted to scream. *Mother, you can't do this!* she projected.

As Lwaxana continued to smile out at her students, she replied, *Of course I can. For years I've toyed with the idea of teaching, really. But now isn't the time to discuss it, Little One. We'll go to lunch after class and I'll tell you all about it.*

Deanna bolted from her chair. *I will not let you do this!*

Lwaxana blinked in surprise. *Deanna Troi, just where do you think you're—*

But the mental query stopped short as Deanna turned her back and headed swiftly for the exit. She was horrified to find Alex Renny seated near the exit

sign. He was in this class, Deanna suddenly remembered. She had been so intent on escaping him that
she'd forgotten he actually had reason to follow her.
"Not telepathic, eh?" he whispered accusingly.

Deanna ignored him and ran out of the room.

"You can go in now." The young ensign opened
the office door and gestured Deanna inside. Deanna
was struck with an urge to run the other way, but of
course she didn't. She stepped over the threshold and
heard the door close softly behind her.

Lieutenant Commander Thaddeus Gold sat behind

his oak desk, crisp and clean, the very picture of efficiency. "Cadet Troi, glad to meet you. Have a seat."

Deanna sat, weighted down by a sense of dread. She didn't need telepathic powers to help her figure out why Gold had summoned her. He was a freshman counselor. Lwaxana had arrived on campus four days earlier. The equation was easy: academic pressure plus empathic overload plus unexpected mother equals one dysfunctional Starfleet cadet.

"So," Gold began, "how are things going?"

"Fine, sir," Deanna replied in a still voice.

Gold picked up a data padd and skimmed a few screens. "Let's see here. . . . Your records show that your entrance exam scores were excellent. Your academic records on Betazed were excellent. Your psych records show you to be bright, energetic, and positive." He put down the little padd and looked her straight in the eye. "Your performance in all areas has suddenly dropped in the past few days, Cadet. I'd like to know what's happening."

Deanna guessed the counselor was already aware of the specifics of her problem. He just wanted her to articulate it first and come up with her own solution, if she could. "I'm having difficulty building my mental shields, sir," she answered. "My . . . my mother warned me about that before I came, but I thought I could handle it. At first I couldn't, but I'm doing better now."

Gold stood up, walked to his fifth-story window, and gazed out. The morning sun hadn't yet burned off the

San Francisco fog, and the city was enveloped in a soft white blanket—except for Starfleet Academy, which, for reasons known only to the winds, lay bathed in crisp sunlight at the moment, a haven of clarity in the fog. "Cadet Troi, why exactly did you enroll in Starfleet Academy?"

A cold dread settled over Deanna, as if something important to her was about to be snatched away. "I want to serve in the Fleet," she replied.

"You haven't declared a major."

"I took several psychology courses at the University of Betazed, sir. I'll probably specialize in psychology here, but I wanted to spend my first year considering options."

Gold turned to face her. "Yet you're in the command track."

An undeclared major in the command track was, to say the least, unusual. "It was a condition of my enrollment that I apply for the command track, sir," Deanna said.

"Whose condition?"

Fighting embarrassment, Deanna answered, "M-my mother's."

Gold nodded. "Deanna, your mother's presence on campus is not a secret."

Under less strenuous circumstances, Deanna would have laughed at that understatement of the year. Lwaxana Troi's presence was never a secret—Lwaxana herself always made sure of that.

Gold's voice took on a note of sympathy, although

his expression remained firm. "I'm sure you're uncomfortable with certain aspects of your mother's new position here, but the fact remains that you have duties to fulfill, and you're not fulfilling them. You have some hard decisions to make, Cadet, the first of which is whether or not you intend to graduate from this institution in four years."

"I do, sir," Deanna blurted out.

"Good. I'd like to see you succeed. Now, I believe that the strength of your mental shields will improve over time. You're not the first to experience such a difficulty. But think—if you can't control your performance around your own mother, how will you perform under the command of a seasoned Starfleet officer in a crisis?"

Anxiety churned in Deanna's stomach, making her feel nauseated. And angry. Angry at a certain new Academy instructor. "I'll learn, sir," she said. "I'll work hard. I'll get back on my feet, I promise."

"I advise you to do so, Cadet. It would be a shame if you washed out before even making it to the *Borocco-Kai.*"

Deanna had already heard about the *Borocco-Kai* test, nicknamed the Big Washout by upperclassmen. It was the first deliberate "thinning-out test" the Academy conducted, a holosuite simulation designed to weed out freshmen who couldn't take the strain of disaster—disaster that might all too easily happen to them as Starfleet officers out in space. The scenario changed every year, but the parameters always remained the same.

Unlike a surprise test, the Big Washout carried the added weight of anticipation. Freshmen had to take it, they knew they had to take it, and they knew it would end in disaster. How they handled it was the key. Unlike the psych test that earned one the right to enter Starfleet Academy, the *Borocco-Kai* test earned a cadet the right to stay there. Failure meant dismissal.

Gold folded his arms, looking at Deanna in such a way that she was suddenly reminded of her father. True, her memories of him were dim, but she could recall him standing just as Gold stood now, arms folded, head slightly tilted, his Starfleet uniform crisp and spotless. For just a moment, Deanna felt that Ian Andrew Troi was there in the room with her, a ghostly aura of warm encouragement. Then the feeling was gone.

Gold picked his computer padd back up, touched several keys, then handed the padd to Deanna. The screen simply read, "Sudak Hall, room 352, 1800 hours."

"That's the time and place to meet your new study group," he said. "Tonight."

Deanna took in the information and handed the padd back. *Study group?* she thought, but all she said was, "Yes, sir."

"I know your empathic powers are making it difficult for you to meet people. This group consists of good students. They should help you focus your energy, and who knows? You might even make a friend or two." Deanna didn't say anything, so Gold nodded to her. "Dismissed, Cadet."

By the time she was outside the building and walking back to her dorm, Deanna was furious. *A study group!* she thought, walking past the beautiful campus rose garden and the sparkling water fountain without even seeing them. *I don't want to be in a stupid study group. I can study just fine on my own. What I need is for everybody to stop giving me advice and just leave me alone!*

At 1800 hours Deanna entered Sudak Hall and found herself alone.

She knew the building was crammed with freshman cadets, but they were all behind closed doors, studying. The deserted halls made her realize just how big the dorm was, how big Starfleet Academy was. *I'm one person here among thousands,* she thought, feeling very small all of a sudden.

When she reached room 352, she braced herself before activating the door chime. Would the study group members like her? Would she be able to keep her shields, and her spirits, up? Or would she be an unwanted intruder in an already established group?

Curious, Deanna carefully lowered her shields, which were a little stronger now. That made her smile—at least something in her life was improving. She allowed the emotions of those in room 352 to filter into her mind. Four beings were in there, all intensely concentrating, no doubt on homework.

Deanna immediately recognized the calm serenity of one particular mind. "Auburn!" she called out.

In seconds the door opened to reveal the Ichthyan, grinning with delight. The three other cadets in the room sat around the table, surrounded by computer padds and stacks of data packs. They stared at Deanna with interest.

"Troi!" Auburn burbled. "You are our new member?"

"Looks like it." Deanna was grinning like a fool, but she didn't care. With Auburn in the picture, this whole study-group nonsense suddenly looked a whole lot more palatable. *Maybe Counselor Gold knows what he's doing after all,* she thought.

And then she saw Alex Renny. He sat across the meeting table from a tall, handsome Xybaki male. "Well, well, well," Renny said without any emotion in his voice. However, Deanna could feel his irritation at her presence.

Deanna put her shields back up fast, for once effectively blocking Renny's emotions before they affected her own. "Hello, Mr. Renny," she replied evenly.

The Xybaki stood up. "Rowrrr," he said with a mischievous grin.

Even through her shields, Deanna sensed the Xybaki's interest in her. She'd never met a native of Xybaka VI before, but she'd heard about them. They were a beautiful people, friendly, intelligent, and they had two hearts—maybe that was why they were known as the galaxy's biggest flirts. "You are a gor-

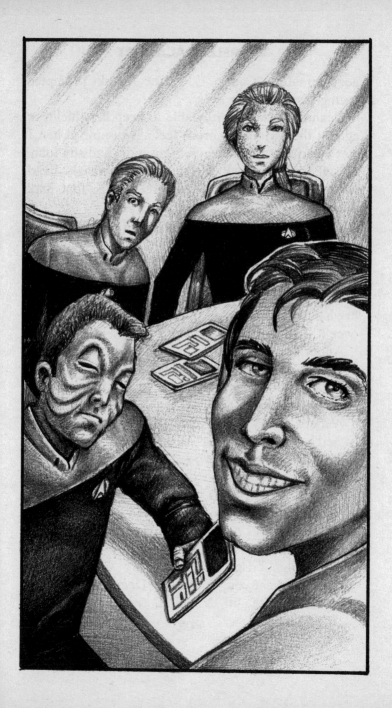

geous creature, Cadet . . . ?" the Xybaki prompted, gazing deep into her eyes.

Deanna blushed, hardly able to keep her shields up against the wave of amorous feelings rushing at her. It was a curious, almost *playful* sensation, and she found herself grinning back at that mind-bogglingly handsome face, those soulful jade-green eyes, that dark, thick, wavy hair and . . .

Deanna shook her head. *Get a hold of yourself!* she thought desperately. With effort she regained her composure and managed to stammer, "Troi . . . I'm Deanna Troi. And you are . . . ?"

"Vandin ua Xadmy Sidk," he murmured, and kissed her hand. "But don't get those luscious lips in a tangle over it. Just call me Vandin."

Auburn snorted, a weird sound Deanna had never heard her make before. It reminded her of a cat sneezing. "You soon may have need to call him *off,*" the Ichthyan said sarcastically.

Auburn gently took Deanna by the shoulders and turned her to face the last member of the study group, a little Zakdorn male who struggled to get up from his cross-legged position on the floor. He was squat and clumsy—Zakdorns weren't built for physical prowess—but he got to his feet and shook Deanna's hand, staring into her face as if cataloging every feature for future reference. "Tronnald First-House," he said in a high, crisp voice.

"Glad to meet you, Tronnald," Deanna replied, still trying to shake off Vandin's smooth-as-chocolate greeting. She dared a glance over at the Xybaki. He was still smiling at her, his jade-green eyes half-lidded and dreamy.

Deanna was relieved to learn that the study group had just formed that week, so her presence wasn't the intrusion she'd feared it would be. Vandin suggested the cadets go around the room and tell each other about themselves. He started it off by saying that he was in the command track "just like you, beautiful Deanna." He considered himself a Kirk-in-training: "I am born to lead; others are born to follow," was his motto. Deanna wasn't sure if she should laugh or be disgusted at this blatant display of ego, so she just kept quiet.

Little Tronnald had gone through two Zakdorn years of medical education before he heard the "mesmerizing call of the cosmos," as he put it. He intended to finish his medical training at Starfleet and practice his art out among the stars.

Alex Renny was a communications major from the state of Oregon here on Earth. He wanted to work in R&D, experimenting with new communications technologies that would someday penetrate the "silent reaches of our galaxy."

And Auburn, Deanna already knew, was in the command track and had definite plans. "Someday I will captain a Galaxy-class starship," she said with quiet certainty. When Vandin laughed at this, she merely turned to him and added, "Or perhaps something bigger."

It was Deanna's turn. "Well, I'm undeclared at the moment," she told the group, "but I am in the command track."

Silence. Then everyone responded at once. "How could you be undeclared?"

"You're kidding!"

"I don't believe it!"

"Boy, are you going nowhere at warp speed!"

Deanna frowned. "What's wrong with being undeclared?" she snapped. Then she caught herself, realizing that her anger was rising for no real reason except that she'd been feeling defensive lately. More calmly she went on, "I studied psychology on Betazed, but I need to make sure that's really what I want to devote my life to. There's so much out there—I'm just too young to know for certain what my future should be."

Vandin vehemently shook his head. "No, no, no, my lovely, that is not the way to go through Starfleet Academy. Goals. You need specific goals."

"Or you'll find yourself shuffled to the side," Tronnald added.

"I am in agreement," stated Auburn, "though I understand Troi's difficulty."

"Telepathy is a difficulty?" Renny asked, not without venom. To the others he explained, "She can read your mind, you know."

Vandin turned to Deanna, intrigued. "Really?" He batted his eyes coyly. "Read mine, my goddess."

"Will you please stop referring to me by such names?" Without waiting for a response, Deanna turned to Renny. "Mr. Renny, how many times do I have to tell you? I'm an *empath,* not a telepath."

"Stow it," Renny said. "I saw you and your mother yakking without saying a word!"

"That was my mother's doing. She's a full Betazoid. It's her powers, not mine, that allow us to talk telepathically. Left on my own, I'm only an empath, and I don't want to have to say it again!"

"You don't have to. I know what I saw!"

"Enough!" Auburn's normally bubbly voice was sharp and clear as she cut through the rising argument. "Alex Renny, I am the roommate of Troi. I know that she cannot read minds." Her words sounded like an order.

Renny backed down, but not without a sulky, "I know what I saw."

"I think we should get some studying done," muttered Tronnald.

"A grand idea, Master Zakdorn," Vandin said cheerfully. "Warp physics, anyone?" He held up a data pack, his expression hopeful.

Deanna was too furious to speak. She could sense Auburn's concern, Renny's anger, and Tronnald's dislike of having a conflict in the group.

Vandin looked from one of them to the next and, with a sigh, tossed the data pack over his shoulder. "Okay, warp physics is out. How about—"

"I need a break." Deanna got up. "Excuse me."

She walked out, feeling everyone's confusion behind her—except Renny, who oozed suspicion in her direction. *Great,* she thought. *This ought to help me just fine. I'm stuck with one cadet who hates me, another who's infatuated with me, another who can't deal with conflict, and a fourth who has to play den mother to us all. And to top it off, they all think they have a right to give* me *advice!*

If the door leading out into the cool night air hadn't been automatic, Deanna would have kicked it open.

CHAPTER

5

Cargo Freighter *BOROCCO-KAI*
Alpha Quadrant, Sector C

Someone viciously kicked the cabin door. Deanna scrambled to her feet as it opened, revealing Captain Chogu's second-in-command. He gestured at her, then at the corridor. "Come now!"

He took her to a cargo locker deep in the bowels of the freighter, pushed her inside, and locked the metal door behind her. The interior of the hold was dark, but Deanna sensed the owner of the voice that cried out, "Troi!"

"Auburn!" A wave of relief washed over Deanna as the Ichthyan's tall figure bounded out of the shadows. The familiar cool hands grasped her shoulders.

"Yes, it is me!" Auburn burbled happily. Then she paused. "Troi, heard you word of the *Chippewa?* Know you of her status?"

Deanna shook her head and told Auburn what had happened to her since the Orions arrived. "It's likely that the Orion ship showed up just to distract the *Chippewa,* to keep her from protecting this freighter. The cargo aboard is their primary interest."

"We felt the engines engage some time ago," came the voice of Tronnald First-House. Deanna whirled to her left, and as her eyes adjusted to the dim light of the single glow strip overhead, she made out the figures of the rest of her away team: Ensign First-House, Ensign Renny, and Ensign Sidk. "The pirates have taken us out of the *Chippewa*'s vicinity. We could be in a whole different sector by now," Tronnald finished.

Deanna barely listened, allowing herself a moment to bask in the presence of her teammates. Whatever came next, at least she wasn't alone anymore. "How long have you been in here?" she asked them.

"Renny and I were caught right away," Tronnald said. Renny growled his displeasure at the announcement, but Tronnald went on, "We planned to hide in one of the loaded cargo bays, but the locks would not open. We ended up stuck out in the corridor when—"

"Oh, shut up already," Renny grumbled.

"Do not feel embarrassment," Auburn told Renny in her gurgly but soothing voice. "We have all been captured. I as well was cornered in a corridor." She reached into her uniform pocket and held up her commbadge. "However, this I managed to hide from them. But it gives no advantage unless we remove the damping field around this vessel."

"I made it as far as sickbay," Vandin said with casual haughtiness. "I gave those pirates a run for their money, I can tell you."

"You still got caught," Renny reminded him.

"Yeah, after taking one of those pirate slugs out

with a hypo full of snooze juice. He'll be dreaming for hours."

So that was it, Deanna thought, remembering the empathic impression she'd gotten earlier that one of the away team members had triumphed, if only for a moment.

"You accomplished a great feat, Mr. Sidk," Auburn said. "There are now five of them and five of us."

"But they're out there and we're in here," Tronnald noted glumly, "without communications or weapons."

Renny shot Tronnald a low-browed look. "Thank you, Mr. Sunshine."

Deanna felt the emotional tone of the group darken. "Okay, so we've all been captured," she said quickly, trying to lighten the mood, "but we're alive, right? I've heard that Orions don't take live captives."

"Sure they do," said Vandin. "They torture the ugly ones and sell the pretty ones at slave auctions." He leaned toward Deanna. "You and I could be sold as a pair. What do you say, O flame of my hearts?"

Before Deanna could respond, Auburn stepped in. "Enough, Mr. Sidk. You will confine your comments to the business at hand."

Vandin regarded Auburn with cold eyes. "Yes, sir, Ensign Twil, sir. But might I remind the group that a little humor now and then eases tension?" He grinned. "Works for me, anyway."

"Let us not lose sight of our mission objective," Auburn told the others, calmly ignoring Vandin. "We have been ordered to secure this vessel and save the crew."

"Then let's bring the pirates in here." Vandin paced back and forth as he spoke, the dim glow strip throwing his shadow against the bulkheads like a restless wraith. "Even if they all come at once, it'll be an even fight."

Auburn shook her head. "Direct confrontation is not our best course."

"Well, sitting here certainly isn't," Vandin shot back.

"We have no weapons effective against disruptors," Auburn insisted.

Vandin tapped his skull. "Then we'll use our brains. Those Orions are bolder than they are smart."

Deanna held her breath as Auburn stepped up to Vandin until her face was mere inches from his. "I am in charge," Auburn stated with calm confidence. "We shall not battle the Orion pirates, and we shall not lure them here. This bay is a prison. We require space to maneuver."

"I think you're playing it too cautious, *sir*," Vandin responded, not as calmly but just as confidently. "If we wait much longer, we'll be too far away from Federation territory to contact anybody, even using the freighter's comm system should we gain access to it." He turned to the group for support.

Once again Deanna felt the emotional tone of the group change, but now it was a dangerous change. Vandin's insubordination was creating incredible tension. *I have to do something,* she thought, *but what?* And then something that had been nagging at the back of her mind for the last few minutes suddenly became clear. "Wait a minute—the air is fresh!" she said. "Smell it!"

Tronnald sniffed. "Troi is right. This could be a hold for biological cargo. If so, that means there's a ventilation system."

"We already looked," Renny insisted. "There are no openings anywhere."

"Then how do you explain the air?" Deanna asked him.

Vandin gracefully swept up Deanna's hand and kissed it before she snatched it back. "My lovely Deanna, there is no vent," he purred in an infuriatingly condescending tone. "Believe me."

"Ensign Sidk, I'll *believe* you when *knowing for certain* ceases to be an option." Deanna wanted to say more—like "And kindly keep your paws to yourself!"—but now was not the time. "Look, the Orions are tricky," she told the others. "If there's a vent system in here, they may have camouflaged it, knowing they'd be using this hold to imprison us."

"Then let us examine all surfaces again, with more care this time," Auburn ordered. She turned to Vandin. "Agreed, Mr. Sidk?"

Deanna watched as Vandin narrowed his eyes and pursed his lips. *He can't stand taking orders from Auburn,* she thought. *He hates not being in charge.* Deanna decided to leave her mental shields lowered

to monitor Vandin as well as the rest of the away team. Leaving her mind vulnerable would hurt, but her empathy might be useful in diffusing further disagreements. *We all have to work together if we're going to get out of this jam,* she thought.

Auburn split the group up, and everyone began to examine every surface of the cargo bay. Within minutes Renny said, "Over here! I thought this was just a nick in the bulkhead before, but maybe it's something more." He was kneeling beyond the range of the glow strip, so all Deanna could see of him was a vague black shape in the shadows.

Auburn started to move toward him, but Vandin pushed past her and reached Renny first. "There's a thin metal plate here, a little less than a meter square," Vandin said, groping along the wall in the dark. "It could be covering something."

"Here." Deanna pulled the clip from her hair and handed it to Renny. "This could help."

After a few minutes of scraping and grunting, Renny and Vandin pried the metal sheet partway off the wall. "Well, whaddaya know?" Renny murmured as a blast of recirculated air blew on them. "Our local mind reader was right! I'm impressed."

Vandin added, "And I'm in love, so I guess that means—"

"Shhh!" Deanna reached out and touched Vandin's shoulder to silence him. Panic was welling up in her, but the feeling didn't belong to her. It was coming from beyond the bulkhead. "Somebody's in there," she whispered.

"In the shaft?" Auburn whispered back from the darkness.

"Yes," Deanna confirmed. "And whoever it is, is heading this way!"

CHAPTER

6

Starfleet Academy
Earth

Whoever it was, she was heading right toward her.

Deanna jumped to her feet and faced the door. She was alone in her dorm room. Auburn had gone for an evening swim, so Deanna was using the time to squeeze in some much needed study. But there'd be no more studying now. "Come in, Mother," she said, recognizing the presence outside.

The door whooshed open and Lwaxana Troi sailed in, the train of her gown rustling after her, the gems in her earrings and hairpiece sparkling in the overhead light. *Little One, how wonderful to see you!* she greeted Deanna telepathically, kissing her cheek. Then she called aloud, "You may enter, Mr. Xelo!"

"Mother, what—" but Deanna got no further as Xelo, Lwaxana's valet, entered with an antigrav serving cart laden with silver dishes and covered serving platters. He nodded pleasantly to her, then began to set solid silver tableware for two on the little study table. "Mother, what in the world is this?" Deanna demanded.

It's dinner. What does it look like? Lwaxana's expression turned to one of alarm. *Don't tell me you've eaten already.* Then she waved her hand in a dismissive gesture. *Well, if you have, you'll still want some of these imported Tribalian spiced prinkets! After our little tiff in class the other morning, I decided the least I could do is bring you a decent meal. Heaven knows what they make you eat here.* Lwaxana glanced about the dorm room as if suddenly seeing it. *What an ugly little room. There should be a law against making people live in closets.*

Deanna nearly exploded. "Mother, explain yourself! And do so out loud, we're not on Betazed anymore."

"No, we're not, are we?" Lwaxana sighed as if the fact depressed her. "Deanna, don't think I haven't noticed how you've been ignoring my calls. I've been on campus for several days now, yet here you are going about your business as if I didn't exist. You and I need to have a little chat." Xelo pulled a chair out for her, and Lwaxana gracefully seated herself. "Please, Little One, sit down."

"I will do no such thing!" All Deanna could think of was the embarrassment of that morning in xenosociology and, worse, the look in Alex Renny's eyes as she'd stormed out of the lecture hall. "How dare you waltz in here with all of this—this—" Deanna gestured helplessly at the catered dinner. Good grief, what if someone had seen Lwaxana enter the dorm? Jokes might already be flying across campus about the freshman whose mother-the-teacher delivered a catered dinner to her dorm room!

"Oh, for heaven's sake," Lwaxana said with a huff. "All right, if you must know, I was just trying to make it easier for you."

Deanna paused, confused. "Easier for me to what?"

"To apologize, of course. You think I'm going to let the other morning go by as if it never happened?"

Deanna was shocked. "You expect *me* to apologize to *you*?"

Lwaxana waved her hand, and Xelo dished out a plump, delicately roasted game bird with squatty little legs—a Tribalian spiced prinket. "That's usually what daughters do when they embarrass their mothers in public," she said.

"*I* embarrassed *you?*" Deanna spluttered. "I don't believe this!"

"Frankly, I don't either. You're away from home for only a couple of weeks and *boom,* your manners go out the window."

It was all Deanna could do not to scream. Balling her fists, she paced the room twice, then decided to sit down before the furious energy raging through her body made her do something unfortunate, like throw a data pack at the wall. "What are you doing here at the Academy, Mother? And don't tell me you've suddenly developed an overwhelming urge to enter the teaching profession."

"Actually, I've been considering it for some time," Lwaxana smoothly replied. "After all, my services as a mother are no longer needed, are they? And since I was here, I thought I might be able to help you."

"Help me?" Deanna stared at her mother. "I—I don't need your help."

"Really? Then explain why your mental shields were failing you, and then explain why they've suddenly become stronger in the past few days."

Deanna backed away. "No," she whispered, a sense of failure gripping her, squeezing the confidence out of her. "No, Mother . . . I thought I was finally . . . No! Don't tell me that support is your doing!"

"Of course it's my doing." Lwaxana daintily carved off a chunk of prinket as she continued, "The moment my shuttle entered orbit around Earth I could feel you struggling down here like a gull in a windstorm. So I reinforced your shields from a distance, and I've been doing so ever since." She pointed her prinket-laden fork at Deanna. "You need me, Little One. I told you that before you left." And she popped the meat into her mouth.

All the independence Deanna had felt since her arrival at the Academy crashed down around her. "Stop it!" she cried out. "Whatever help you're giving me with my mental shields, just stop! Mother, I'll never grow up if you don't let me!"

Lwaxana shrugged and, for just a moment, her eyes grew distant. Then, like water crashing through a broken dam, a flood of emotions crashed into Deanna's head, a maelstrom of anger and joy and jealousy and rage and everything in between. Deanna reeled as the last of Lwaxana's supporting power was pulled away from her.

She grabbed her head and, closing her eyes, concentrated as she'd never concentrated before. This was the crucial test: if she couldn't regain control of her shields here, in front of her mother, she'd never do it. She could feel Lwaxana watching her and, after a moment of struggling, her thoughts cleared. She drew in a shuddering breath.

"Good," Lwaxana admitted. "Not great, but good. You need practice."

"I've been practicing," Deanna said with effort. A pounding headache throbbed at her temples, but she was determined to hide it.

You can't hide anything from me, Little One, you know that, Lwaxana said telepathically. *You might as well admit the truth.*

"That's it!" Deanna stood up and jabbed a finger at the door. "Please leave!"

"What? Deanna, how dare you—"

"Leave, Mother! I'm going to grow up whether you want me to or not. I'm going to succeed here at the

Academy, and I'm going to show you that I don't need your help or anybody else's anymore. Now, please, I have studying to do."

Slowly, with great dignity, Lwaxana rose from her chair. "Mr. Xelo," she said, "you may clean up."

In a flurry of motion, Xelo cleared off the study table and loaded everything back onto the antigrav cart. Deanna watched as he hastened out the door.

We'll continue this discussion later, Little One, Lwaxana said telepathically, and followed him out.

Deanna managed to control herself for thirty seconds before she did something unfortunate—she threw a data pack at the wall.

It broke.

CHAPTER

7

Cargo Freighter *BOROCCO-KAI*
Alpha Quadrant, Sector C

The ventilation grille broke free of the bulkhead and
crashed to the cargo bay floor. Deanna jumped back
in surprise, and judging by the scuffling sounds in the
darkness around her, her away team members did the
same. She felt new emotions in the cargo bay now—
terror, determination, and a desperate defiance.

"Get back!" ordered a man's voice. It was edged
with hysteria. "I've got a phaser!"

Deanna felt her comrades gather themselves, ready
to fight. "It's all right," she said quickly but calmly.
"Everybody just relax. Our new friend isn't Orion."

Indeed, though she couldn't see him, Deanna sensed the unmistakable human quality of his emotions.

"Who are you?" Vandin demanded of the unseen newcomer.

"I've got a phaser!" the voice repeated frantically. "I'll use it!"

Deanna grabbed Vandin's arm and squeezed, hoping he'd get the message to keep quiet. "Yes, you have a phaser," she said slowly to their newcomer. "But you don't want to use it on us. We're Starfleet officers, here to help you."

"You're . . . Starfleet?"

"Yes. We'll show you. We'll move into the light."

Deanna headed back into the hazy light from the overhead glow strip, and the others followed. "See our uniforms?" Deanna called out. "You can come out now."

Something shifted and scraped in the shadows, and then a figure limped into view. "My leg," the man groaned. "It's cut pretty bad."

Tronnald rushed forward. "I'm a medic. Allow me to help."

As Tronnald went to work, Deanna studied the newcomer. He was a middle-aged human dressed in a filthy, torn work tunic. Clearly he'd fought against the Orions; his face and arms were covered with cuts and bruises, and his left thigh was bleeding from a knife wound. Tronnald gently probed the cut. "Ouch!" The man waved his phaser around as he squirmed in pain.

"Please!" cried Auburn, dodging the wild aim. "Put down your weapon!"

The man obeyed. "There's nothing to worry about. This phaser is empty. I used up the energy cell hours ago."

Vandin scooped the phaser up. "You were bluffing?" He grinned. "Excellent! We fell for it!"

"That's not something I'd brag about," Deanna said.

Pocketing the phaser, Vandin gave his reply as if explaining a simple principle that even an infant could understand. "All it takes, my gorgeous princess, is attitude. If you've got that, a bluff can be your best weapon."

"Unless your opponent has equal attitude," countered Renny, "in which case your opponent calls your bluff and you, my friend, are hash."

Deanna regarded Renny with surprise. He had come to her aid, siding with her against Vandin. Curious.

Tronnald cut any more bickering short. "I need some cloth, enough to pad and bandage this wound."

Without a moment's hesitation, Auburn ripped off one sleeve of her uniform, then the other, biting some of the stubborn threads loose with her sharp teeth. "I confess a dislike of long sleeves," she stated in her matter-of-fact way. "They restrict movement."

"Perfect!" Tronnald said, taking the severed sleeves.

The stranger nodded at Auburn. "Thank you, uh . . ."

"Ensign Twil d-ch-Ka," Auburn offered. She then introduced the others.

"I'm Bodrik Denburgh, ship's engineer."

"What were you doing in the ventilation shaft?" asked Deanna.

"Hiding, what do you think?" Denburgh shook his head, anguished. "As far as I know, I'm the only one they haven't captured yet."

"You are the first civilian we have seen," Auburn told him. "Status of your shipmates?"

Denburgh shuddered, and Deanna was hit by a fresh

wave of fear. "I don't know. I saw . . . they . . ." He couldn't go on.

Deanna barely fortified her mental shields in time to protect herself as Denburgh's mind overflowed with emotion. *Poor man,* she thought. *He has nothing to protect himself from the power of his own memories.* She knelt down next to him. "It's all right," she said, taking his hand in hers. "You're safe now. Just tell us where your shipmates are."

"Some are dead," Denburgh finally said, "but their bodies are gone. The Orions probably . . . probably threw them out the airlock." If he noticed Deanna shudder, he didn't acknowledge it. "All the rest were rounded up and locked in a cargo pod." Denburgh looked in desperation first at Auburn, then at Deanna. "Is it true? Do Orions sell people as slaves?"

"Do not worry," Auburn said, investing her voice with as much authority as she could. It worked. Denburgh calmed down as if he'd been commanded to do so by a superior officer. "We are alive, and we will do all possible to aid your shipmates."

"You're too late," the engineer moaned. "The Orions have already taken the *Borocco-Kai* out of the system. We lost contact with the *Chippewa* long ago."

A horrible thought occurred to Deanna, and Tronnald's emotions told her that he was thinking the same thing. The Zakdorn gave voice to it first: "Do you think the *Chippewa* fought the Orions . . . and lost?"

Auburn squared her shoulders. "We will proceed as if the *Chippewa* is delayed only. Our orders are clear:

66

save the civilians. Save the ship, if possible." With a nod to Denburgh, she continued, "We have now a route of escape from this prison."

"Wait, I took that route to get *in* here," Denburgh said. "I just want to hide in a dark corner, and if you're smart, you'll do the same. If we start running around out there, they'll hunt us down."

"Not me, chum," said Vandin. *"I'm* the one who's going hunting."

"And we have orders to obey." Auburn gestured the others to their feet. "We will attack."

"Whoa!" said Renny. "Ten minutes ago you argued *against* attack."

"Ten minutes ago we were trapped," Deanna reminded him, "and ten minutes ago we didn't have a ship's engineer to help us."

"Help you?" Denburgh cried in alarm.

"Deanna is correct," said Auburn before Denburgh could protest further. "We must move with speed."

Vandin faced Auburn, grinning. "Now you're talkin', sir!"

Auburn grinned back at him. "See you now that I fear not to fight?" she said, her bubbly voice filled with anticipation. "I merely avoid confrontation until I have a good chance to *win*."

CHAPTER

8

Starfleet Academy
Earth

This meeting wasn't going to be like the first one. This
would be more like a battle—a battle she had to win.

Deanna stepped into Thaddeus Gold's office and
stood at attention. The counselor, sitting behind his
desk, finally looked up from the padd he'd been reading. "Cadet Troi," he greeted her. "As you were.
What can I do for you?"

Deanna relaxed her stance, nervously clearing her
throat. "First of all, sir, I would like to thank you for
seeing me without an appointment."

"Your request sounded . . . important."

Deanna nodded. "Yes, sir. To me it is." *Just spit it out, Deanna!* "Sir, I'd like to sign up to take the *Borocco-Kai* simulation."

Lieutenant Commander Gold was far too professional to do a bug-eyed double take at Deanna's announcement. Yet something in the way he blinked had almost the same effect. "Really?"

"Yes, sir."

Gold seemed to weigh several factors in his mind. Then he said, "You do have the right to take the test at any time during your freshman year, though most cadets choose to do so at the end of their second semester. They want to learn all they can from their classes, in case the knowledge and skills gained are necessary during the simulation."

"I am aware of that, sir."

"Are you also aware that if you fail, you will be dismissed from the Academy?"

"Yes, sir, I am."

Gold nodded. "Then tell me—why are you so eager to put yourself on the line?"

Deanna had the answer ready. She'd practiced every possible version of this meeting in her mind for the past hour, knowing that this one question would be unavoidable. "I thought about what you said during our last meeting, sir. You were right, of course; I do have some hard decisions to make. Well, I've made some of them. Until now I've been letting certain . . . aspects of my life intimidate me. Instead of protecting myself by building up my own mental shields, I've been blaming other beings for having emotions. Instead of controlling my empathic abilities and reaching out to others in friendship, I've been holding back and then feeling angry that others aren't reaching out to me." Deanna shrugged. "Simple mistakes, sir, but they were revelations to me."

Gold gave her a little smile. "Cadet, there is nothing simple about personal relationships. In fact, the simplest social skills are often the hardest to master because everyone assumes they should come naturally. Nobody's born with the automatic ability to get along with others, however. It's a learned skill. Unfortunately, not everyone learns it." His smile faded, and he leaned back in his chair. "About the *Borocco-Kai* test, however—"

"It's the solution to my final problem, sir," Deanna stated.

"Final problem?"

He already knows, Deanna reminded herself. *He must know. He's just making you say it yourself.* "My ability to make decisions, sir. I have recently learned that some decisions, even when made, carry no weight if they're not accepted by others."

"That's called lack of authority," Gold offered.

"Exactly," agreed Deanna. "Without authority, people can make all the decisions they want, but it won't do them any good."

Deanna paused, anguished. *I can't do it. I can't complain to him about my own mother. I just can't talk about her behind her back, no matter what the circum-*

stances. There must be another way! But no other way came to mind.

Gold waited as if he knew exactly what kind of war was going on in Deanna's head. When she didn't speak, he said, "Authority comes with experience, doesn't it?"

The question came out of nowhere. "Yes, sir," Deanna answered, wondering.

But Gold said no more. He just folded his arms and looked at her, his expression neutral.

And then Deanna understood. *He's giving me an opening.*

"Experience is the key," she began, groping for the right words. "For instance, I made the decision to come to the Academy, but I'm not moving forward, as you pointed out before. I need to gain authority in order to back up my own decisions. I need to prove to"—*be honest, Deanna!*—"to myself most of all that my decision to come here was the right decision." She tried not to plead, but she couldn't help it. "Sir, let me take the *Borocco-Kai* test. If I'm meant to be here, I'll pass. And I know that when I do, everything else will fall into place."

Gold scratched the lobe of one ear in a contemplative gesture. "An all-or-nothing plunge, hm? You know that you can't take the test alone. You'll need a team of at least two other cadets, preferably three. I don't think you're going to find many freshmen willing to jeopardize their careers this early."

"I'll find them somehow, sir."

Gold gave her a wry look. "Yes, I bet you will." He stood up. "Very well. Cadet Troi, I grant you permission to sign up for the test."

Deanna couldn't hold back her relief. "Thank you, sir."

"Don't thank me," Gold warned. "I think this is foolish of you, and I want you to tell any cadets who consider teaming up with you to talk with me first. This isn't your gamble alone."

Deanna thought the meeting was over, but Gold walked her to the door. "I wouldn't give such permission to just anyone, Cadet—understand that. But I'm well aware of your situation." He paused, choosing his words carefully. "You see, when your mother came to campus, I made it my business to meet her. She is a most beautiful, charming, and extraordinarily strong-willed woman."

Deanna felt several emotions flit by—respect, amusement, irritation, admiration—Gold's emotions toward her mother. She tried not to grin. "Yes, sir. That she is."

Gold opened the door. "The rules for the test are available through your computer uplink, Cadet. Read them carefully and be ready to report to Training Holosuite Four in three days."

"Yes, sir!"

"I plan to take the *Borocco-Kai* simulation test in three days," Deanna announced to her study group that night.

She'd walked into the Sudak Hall study area well prepared to say those words. And though it was the exact opposite of what she'd been trying to do for the past three weeks, now she kept her mental shields down and her mind wide open. Deanna wanted to sense every emotion from the cadets in her group.

Auburn, Renny, Vandin, and Tronnald were seated at a round table with their noses buried in class materials. At Deanna's announcement, their heads jerked up and their response came in perfect unison: *"What?"*

"You heard me. I'm going to take the Big Washout."

"But . . . why?" Tronnald asked, mystified. "You don't have to take it—"

"Until second semester, I know. I have my reasons. And I have a reason for telling all of you." Deanna paused. "I can't take it alone. I need a team."

Nobody spoke. Then Auburn's face broke into a wide grin, matching the excitement that Deanna sensed welling up inside her. "Yes! It will make Academy history! To pass the *Borocco-Kai* so early would put distinctions on my permanent record. I wish such a distinction!"

"You're bugnuts," Renny declared uneasily. "This particular distinction is only good if you *pass* the test. What if you flunk?"

Auburn turned her large ocean-blue eyes on Renny. "I will not flunk."

"The test isn't called the Big Washout for nothing," said Tronnald.

Vandin got up from his chair and draped a chummy arm around Deanna's shoulders. "Well, I'd never let you go alone, my pet. I shall come to protect you!"

If Vandin hadn't been serious he would have been hilarious. As it was, Deanna wanted to slug him. "Your sexist gallantry is several centuries out of date, Mr. Sidk, and besides, your *pet* doesn't need a protector." She stepped out from under his arm. "However, if you can behave yourself, I'll *consider* you for the team."

"*My* team," Vandin corrected. "You ladies need a leader."

"Oh, come off it, Sidk," Renny said in disbelief. "You don't even know what the test scenario will be."

"Doesn't matter. I'm best qualified to lead."

"Excuse me," Deanna broke in, "but deciding who will lead is not a priority." The fact was, she didn't want Vandin involved at all, but she couldn't be choosy. She needed him. Renny didn't seem a likely candidate, and Tronnald was shivering at the very idea of the *Borocco-Kai*.

"You know, the queen of my hearts is correct," Vandin agreed. "Leading isn't the issue here—that's already settled. The issue now is teamwork." He gazed from one face to another. "We're all exceptional students, aren't we? We all have high goals, don't we? Why don't we turn the Academy upside down together?"

Tronnald's response was immediate and emphatic: "No!"

"Oh, be quiet, you're coming," Vandin told him flatly.

"But what if we—" Renny began.

"We won't," Auburn assured him.

Deanna could hardly believe it. Even if Renny and Tronnald backed out, she could take the test with Auburn and Vandin. And something in the way Tronnald fidgeted and in the way Renny glowered told her that they were fighting their own fear more than anything else. Perhaps they would change their minds. She could already sense their growing interest. *I've got a team!* Deanna thought gleefully. *I've won half the battle already!*

You haven't even stepped onto the battlefield yet, Little One, came a mental voice.

Deanna gasped. "Mother!"

"Where?" asked Vandin, glancing around the room.

The door of the study hall *whooshed* open, and Lwaxana Troi burst in, an expression of panic on her face. *Is it true, Little One? Are you taking that Washout ordeal in three days?*

Deanna regarded her mother as the other members of her study group regarded Deanna. "Mother, what are you doing here?"

I've come to stop you from making a fool of yourself!

"Speak out loud, Mother. My study group is composed of non-telepaths." Deanna glanced at Renny. "That includes me."

Lwaxana gave her daughter a strange look, then waved a dismissive hand at the other cadets. *This doesn't concern them. I'm speaking to you. You are not taking that test!* Deanna turned her back, and Lwaxana's eyes blazed with outrage. "Very well! I'll say it out loud: You are *not* taking that test!"

"Yes, Mother, I *am* taking that test," Deanna responded, her back still turned.

Lwaxana glared at the other cadets. "You put her up to this, didn't you? Go on, admit it! I can find out on my own, you know." She suddenly turned to Renny and frowned. "How dare you accuse my daughter of such a thing!"

Renny blanched. "What did I say?"

"You don't have to say anything, Mr. Renny," Lwaxana stated. "I am a telepath. And I'll have you know that my daughter is the most honest creature on this planet." She whirled on Vandin. "And you!"

Vandin flinched just a little. "Ma'am?"

"Don't you ma'am me, you—you—" Lwaxana's hands spiraled in front of her as if she were groping for a word out of thin air— "you hormonal wild man! Stay away from my daughter. Is that clear?"

Deanna whirled to face her mother. "Enough, Mother! You're not going to get your way by badgering innocent bystanders!"

"Innocent bystanders? Ha! Little One, these hooligans have encouraged you to throw away your career—especially this one!" and she jabbed an accusing finger at Auburn.

Auburn gazed placidly at Lwaxana as if everything were hunky-dory. "We will leave," the Ichthyan offered, "for you to speak to Deanna with privacy." She gestured the other cadets to the door.

Lwaxana folded her arms. "Fine. You're all dismissed." They hastened out.

"I can't believe you did that." Deanna could barely keep back tears of frustration. "Don't you care how I feel about anything?"

Deanna expected an outburst as a reply, but Lwaxana, always unpredictable, now regarded her daughter with an almost desperate expression. *I might ask you the same question, Little One.* She held up her hands when Deanna started to protest. "All right, all right, I'll talk out loud." She collapsed into a chair with infinite weariness. "You can't imagine what it's been like, Deanna. First I watch you leave Betazed, your birth world, to start a whole new life on a different planet. Then, when I surprise you with my own arrival, you greet me with all the warmth of a Gazedon spit lizard greeting a hungry hawk. I thought you would be pleased to see me! Instead, after I traveled all the way here, what did you do? You rejected me in public, avoided my calls, and threw me out of your room! And now you intend to toss your future away on a childish move designed just to spite me." She waggled a finger at Deanna. "And it is just to spite me, don't deny it."

"Mother, that's not fair. There's more to it than that."

"Don't you think I know what you're doing? You're looking at this test as some kind of Kikabu tribal maturity rite or something. You think if you pass, I'll consider you a full-fledged adult. For heaven's sake, Little One, this test isn't a game—it will determine the rest of your life!"

Deanna burned with embarrassment. She hated it when her mother figured out her strategy. On the other hand, she was used to dealing with telepaths. "I'm aware of all that, Mother. But what else would you have me do?"

"I don't know, but I'll tell you one thing—I didn't come all the way from Betazed to watch you throw your career away."

"You didn't come all the way from Betazed to watch me succeed at it, either."

Lwaxana tensed up, and Deanna feared the argument was about to rise to new heights. But then Lwaxana just laughed, shaking her head in amazement. "You sound just like your father, do you know that?" Her eyes grew distant as she remembered earlier times, before Deanna was born. "Oh, the arguments we had when he was assigned to dangerous missions. I'd try to talk him into resigning from Starfleet, and he'd give me a list of reasons a kilometer long why he had to stay in. I suppose I was jealous. Imagine that—me jealous of Starfleet! But it was all right as long as he came back to me." Her next words were barely above a whisper. "And then one day he *didn't* come back." She grew quiet.

"Mother . . . is that what you think? That I'll go off on some mission and"—the words stuck in Deanna's throat—"get killed?"

Lwaxana's mood made another sudden swing, and now she spoke in a light, casual tone. "Whatever gave you such an idea? Of course not. But your sudden decision to take this test so early . . . well, if you make such a rash decision now, what in heaven might you do when you're an officer?"

Deanna shrugged. "I'll do what my superior officers tell me to do."

"Really?" A shadow of irritation darkened Lwaxana's features. "How very interesting. You're eager enough to obey complete strangers, but you balk at the very thought of obeying me!"

"Mother, Starfleet is different."

"How?" Lwaxana demanded. "How is it different? Starfleet is Starfleet. I'm your *mother!*"

Deanna stared up at the ceiling, fighting to maintain control. If her mother's concerns hadn't been genuine she could have disregarded them. But Lwaxana's love enveloped Deanna in an empathic cloud so thick she felt as if she were choking. *Love is one thing,* she finally decided, *but what she wants is my obedience for the rest of my life. I just can't give her that!* "Mother, I'm going to take the test."

Lwaxana smacked the table with the palm of her hand, making Deanna jump. "You haven't listened to a word I've said, have you, young lady?" Lwaxana gathered up her skirts and headed for the door. "Fine. Do whatever you want. What do I know? I'm just your mother."

And she left.

Deanna's eyes burned and tears threatened to spill down her cheeks. Now she *had* to pass the test. Everything—absolutely everything—depended on it.

CHAPTER

9

Cargo Freighter *BOROCCO-KAI*
Alpha Quadrant, Sector C

"Everything depends on timing," Vandin told the group. They sat under the glow strip in the cargo bay trying to come up with a plan. Everyone had contributed ideas, and now Vandin was stating their final decision. "Okay, so we'll split into two teams. Team one," and he pointed to himself, Auburn, and Deanna, "will head for the bridge. If we're lucky, most if not all of the pirates will be in there. We'll bring down the blast doors, lock the pirates inside, then cut power to the bridge systems. Bye-bye Orion threat."

Auburn nodded approval of the summation thus far.

She had wisely allowed Vandin to take the floor—after all, it was impossible to shut him up—but she interjected comments or questions, pointedly maintaining her authority over the team. Deanna admired the tactic.

"Now, while we're doing that, the rest of you"—Vandin indicated Renny, Tronnald, and Denburgh, the freighter's engineer—"will go to the pod bay on deck twelve. That's where the crew is being held. Denburgh, you said they're in a cargo pod that's code-locked, so we can't get in and they can't get out?"

Denburgh nodded. "Our only option is to detach the pod from the ship. We'll be fine as long as we each have a cargo clamp. If we attach the clamp to a latch or docking hook on the pod's exterior, there's no way we'll come loose. When the pod breaks away, we'll just float along with it. Our emergency environmental suits will protect us in open space."

"For how long?" Renny asked.

"Long enough," Auburn assured him.

"Right," said Vandin. "So we'll attach ourselves to the exterior of the pod with cargo clamps and ride right out with it. Once we get beyond the damping field, we'll contact the *Chippewa* with Auburn's commbadge."

"If the *Chippewa* is not out of range," Auburn gurgled. "That is yet unknown."

"Let's rig a power booster," suggested Renny, "something small and portable."

"Excellent!" Vandin said. "So the pirates won't be

able to recover the pod, fire at it, or even follow it, since they'll be locked on the bridge with no power. We'll contact the *Chippewa,* they'll come and get us, end of story." He spread his arms. "The good guys win!"

The others voiced their approval of the plan. *Vandin may be a nuisance,* thought Deanna, *but he can sure raise morale.*

As Vandin, Deanna, and Auburn prepared for their dangerous journey to the bridge, Renny pulled Vandin aside. Deanna heard him whisper, "Just one thing, fearless not-leader—what are you going to do if the pirates shoot at you?"

Vandin shrugged. "Let's hope they don't."

Moments later Team One walked away from the hazy light of the glow strip, heading back into the dark corner where the ventilation shaft lay open and waiting. Deanna had never suffered from claustrophobia, but she had a feeling the next ten minutes would give her a good taste of it.

Crawling through the shaft wasn't as bad as she expected, but it was still difficult. She had to crawl with a lizardlike motion that scraped her elbows and knees. Because Vandin's body was bigger, he had to hold his arms straight out in front of him, as Denburgh had done, and maneuver with his feet. As for Auburn, she slithered along like a fish through water. She'd gone into the shaft first and was already far ahead. "This shaft terminates approximately ten meters ahead," she whispered back at them.

Deanna had entered last, so by the time she tumbled out of the shaft, Auburn was rested and Vandin was catching his breath. Both of them were filthy and disheveled. No doubt she looked as scraggly as they did.

Brushing her hair out of her eyes, Deanna looked around. The shaft led out into a corridor, as Denburgh had told them. This corridor connected to the main passageway that ran through the center of the freighter and eventually led to the bridge. Auburn silently gestured them forward, but Deanna hung back, concentrating. "Sense you if all the Orions are ahead?" Auburn whispered.

Deanna shook her head. "No, I can't feel the Orions at all."

Auburn pointed to a corridor on their left. "Then let us check sickbay. We cannot forget the pirate drugged by Vandin. It is doubtful he still sleeps, but we must be sure."

Sickbay was empty. They searched each examination booth and even opened the quarantine tank, but did not find the drugged pirate. "He must have awakened and rejoined his fellows. We will assume he is on the bridge," said Auburn.

"Hope he's got a headache the size of a supernova," Vandin growled, finding the empty hypospray he'd used on the Orion.

"Wait a minute." Deanna examined the hypospray. "Is there any more of this drug? We don't have any other weapons, so—"

"An excellent idea." Auburn threw open a cabinet door and rummaged around inside. "Search for more."

They found one more vial of the sleeping drug and reloaded the hypospray. Auburn was about to hand it to Vandin when the Xybaki said gallantly, "I will do without so that my sweet Deanna may—"

"Take it, Xybaki," Auburn ordered, shoving it into his hand. "You now will protect us poor and feeble females."

Rolling his eyes, Vandin accepted the hypospray. "Aye, sir." Then he whispered into Deanna's ear, "You're safe with me, my blossom."

"Funny," she replied coolly, "I feel just the opposite."

"Ah, that's what I adore about you," Vandin purred. "You've got spunk."

Now it was Deanna's turn to roll her eyes. She followed Auburn out of sickbay.

When they reached the bridge, the main door was closed. *Good,* Deanna thought. *They won't be able to see us, and if we're quiet, they won't hear us.* Auburn looked at her and tapped her forehead. Deanna concentrated for a moment, then shook her head. Vandin mouthed, "I'll guard," and took position right outside the closed bridge door as Auburn slowly, quietly opened the control box several meters away.

Deanna was relieved to find that she understood the maze of wires and circuits in the control box. She pinched an impossibly thin, delicate blue wire, indicating that she believed it was part of the blast door controls. Auburn nodded agreement and traced the

85

wire to its connection point within a bundle of other wires. They all merged into a thick insulated cable that disappeared into the bulkhead, where it eventually ran all the way to the ship's main computer.

Before pulling the wire, Auburn and Deanna both looked over to Vandin for an all-clear sign. What they saw shocked them: Vandin's hand was poised to activate the bridge doors! Before they could utter a sound, he slapped the control touchplate, the bridge doors sprang apart, and he leaped through, brandishing the empty phaser he'd gotten from Denburgh. "Fool!" Auburn hissed.

From her angle, Deanna could no longer see Vandin, but she knew what he was trying to do.

"Okay, Orion scum, throw down your weapons!" came his voice, brimming with authority and confidence. "You're surrounded!" Barely were the words out of his mouth when the shrill whine of an Orion disruptor split the air.

Vandin screamed, then his voice simply stopped. Something thudded to the floor, and Denburgh's phaser and the hypospray skittered out the door and into the corridor.

"No!" Deanna cried.

Auburn yanked the blue wire free. The control panel sparked, and the bridge doors slammed shut— but not before one Orion slipped through. He glanced behind him to see the blast doors slam down over the main doors, separating him from his comrades. He raised his disruptor. *"Sh'kilu tze!"* he yelled at Deanna. Then he fired.

Deanna threw herself to one side as the disruptor beam sliced through the air just inches past her shoulder. Behind her, part of the bulkhead exploded, and when she looked up, the Orion was aiming at her again, his yellow teeth bared.

But he never fired. Like a furious tiger, Auburn leaped on him. The Orion obviously hadn't expected such an aggressive act from a female. He went over backward, and Auburn pinned his arms down, her body slim and fragile-looking next to his stocky bulk. Deanna was amazed at the Ichthyan's strength. Though the pirate tried madly to throw her off, he couldn't do it!

Deanna grabbed her chance. Like an old-time baseball player diving for home, she launched herself at the fallen hypospray. Through his struggles with Auburn the Orion saw what she was going for and tried to grab the hypospray first, but Deanna beat him to it. "Take that!" she cried, pressing the instrument against his arm. One quick hiss and the Orion's body went limp. He began to snore.

Auburn scrambled to her feet. "My thanks," she panted. "Let us go!" Only then did Deanna hear the electrical whine of a cutting tool on the opposite side of the bridge doors. A small glowing yellow spot appeared in the center of the door and began to grow. "Troi, they are cutting through! We must hurry!"

"But the bridge power—"

"No time," Auburn said. "We must go *now!*"

Deanna glanced at the phaser lying on the deck. "Vandin—"

But Auburn just grabbed her arm and pulled. Deanna had to take a step to keep from falling. One step, another step—in seconds she was running down the corridor as fast as she could, barely keeping up with Auburn's swift pace. Deanna expected to hear the Orions' footsteps behind her at any moment, but she knew it would take them a long time to cut through the blast doors. She and Auburn made it to the pod bay without mishap.

"We have failed," Auburn panted to the others gathered there. "Vandin, the fool—"

"He tried to bluff the Orions," Deanna added, gasping for breath. "He's dead, and we didn't have time to shut off the bridge power!"

Tronnald and Renny froze in shock, but Denburgh simply reported, "The pod is ready for launch, but we have a little problem. The Orions have taken the environmental suits."

"What?" Deanna cried.

"Don't panic," Denburgh went on. "They missed one storage locker and there are four suits in there."

But there are five of us! Deanna's brain shrilled. Before she could say it out loud, the ship's computerized emergency klaxon began to wail.

"Emergency alert. Emergency alert," intoned the computer's bland, impersonal voice. "All personnel to emergency evacuation stations. Shipwide decompression commencing in four minutes."

CHAPTER

10

Starfleet Academy
Earth

"Four minutes to start of *Borocco-Kai* simulation," announced the computer's bland voice.

Deanna heard those words, and panic gnawed at her stomach. *I'm really doing this. I must be crazy!* She struggled to compose herself, thinking, *Thank goodness I'm the only empath here. Nobody can tell how scared I am.*

She was standing in the soundproof waiting room outside Training Holosuite Four. Behind her in the corridor, a crowd of cadets had gathered to watch the five freshmen flout tradition and take the Big Washout early. Most of the observers were fellow freshmen, but there were cadets of all levels out there, watching curiously through the window. "News travels fast," Vandin had noted on his way in.

Deanna could feel the roiling emotions of the cadets in the crowd. Many radiated envy—not envy at her supposed daring, but envy that she would get the dreaded test over with so soon. Most of the upper-classmen thought she was foolish, but a few of them were actually jealous. "I'd have taken it early, too, if I'd known I could," one junior had told her.

Perhaps so, Deanna thought. *But probably not. They all think I'm doing this to show off. At least Commander Gold understands my reasons.* And she doubted very much if he'd let any other freshman follow in her footsteps—not without equally good reasons.

Deanna glanced at her teammates, who all wore the same test uniform she did. *Whatever the scenario is, we're all ensigns in it,* she thought, absently fingering the single pip at her collar. Each team member also had a tricorder and phaser. *What's going to happen to us in there?*

Auburn looked as if the mystery didn't interest her. She just stood calmly waiting for the holosuite doors to open. Vandin's lips curved upward ever so slightly, as if he looked forward to the test but was trying not to show it. Renny, who'd finally decided to take the test when campus opinion had dubbed Deanna's team "the Sizzlin' Redhots," was chewing his lower lip nervously. And Tronnald, who'd decided to come because, he said, "I'm a lot more adventurous than you think I am!" stood to one side trying desperately not to tremble.

They were all lucky—they couldn't empathically feel the crowd outside. Only Deanna could, and she could feel her teammates' fear as well. Yet despite that fear, she sensed a firm conviction in each of her comrades. *They're ready,* she thought with an unexpected sense of pride. *We're ready.*

"I'll go in first," Vandin told the group in a quiet voice.

Renny shot him a look. "Jeez, are you still trying to play fearless leader?"

"He's been studying Kirk's command records again," Deanna whispered.

Vandin refused to be baited. "Hey, study the best to be the best, beautiful."

Deanna bristled. If Vandin had just made his remark, she would have been able to let it go. But his constant use of "beautiful" and "pet" and all those other names was becoming tiresome. She opened her mouth to retort, but then a cool hand touched her arm and she turned to find Auburn gazing intently at her.

The Ichthyan removed her hand without speaking, but Deanna got the message. *Auburn's right—it's not my job to teach Vandin a lesson. Life will do that for him eventually.*

The holosuite doors *shoofed* open. "Enter," commanded the computer. Vandin shot forward, followed by the others. As Deanna stepped through last, one of her father's sayings flashed through her mind: "May Lady Fortune smile on us all."

Deanna found herself standing on the bridge of a starship. She studied the new surroundings quickly, trying to glean as much information as possible before the action started. *This is a Miranda-class starship,* she thought, *small, crew compliment of 320, introduced in the late twenty-third century.* She glanced at the ship's dedication plaque: *U.S.S. Chippewa.* There was no such ship in the fleet, past or present. This scenario was going to be made up, then, not based on a historical event.

The ship's captain rose from her command chair as the test team entered. Raising her head slightly, she said, "Transporter Room, are you standing by?"

"Aye, Transporter Room standing by, Captain Tallerday," came a male voice over the intercom.

Tallerday is an imaginary captain as well, Deanna thought.

Tallerday faced them. "This is a rescue mission, people. We've intercepted a distress call from the freighter *Borocco-Kai,* a multi-species ship with Alpha Centurian registration. We have no idea what's happened to her, but sensors show hull damage. Let's presume there are casualties aboard, probably a variety of races." She glanced at Tronnald. "Stabilize the injured for immediate transport to our sickbay." Her gaze shifted to the rest of them in turn. "Find out what's going on over there and be quick about it. If the *Borocco-Kai* was attacked, we could be a target as well." She pointed. "You're in charge"—puffing out his chest and radiating ego, Vandin started to step forward—"Ensign d-ch-Ka," Tallerday finished.

Vandin froze. Deanna felt his ego deflate like a pricked balloon.

"Aye, sir!" Auburn bubbled to Tallerday.

The captain nodded curtly and took a step back. "Stand ready, team. We'll transport you immediately, site-to-site. Transporter Room, energize!"

The shimmer of a transporter beam appeared around them. Deanna had certainly used a transporter before, but this was her first journey into the unknown. *May Lady Fortune smile on us all,* she thought again as the bridge faded away.

CHAPTER

11

Cargo Freighter *BOROCCO-KAI*
Alpha Quadrant, Sector C

Deanna felt all hope fade away as the *Borocco-Kai*'s computer announced, "Three minutes, forty-five seconds to shipwide decompression." The freighter's computerized environmental system was going to plunge them into deadly vacuum!

"The Orions know we're trying to escape, and they know they can't cut their way through the blast doors in time to stop us," Deanna said over the blare of the klaxon. "They must have taken the environmental suits for themselves when they boarded the ship."

"Then they've used this tactic before," Renny realized. "Blast, why didn't we see it coming?"

"Look, all that matters is that we've got five people and four suits!" squealed Tronnald. "What do we do?"

"Attention!" Auburn barked. Her command had the desired effect—the others turned their attention to her. "We have minutes left only. Listen and obey. Denburgh, does the pod's launch system still operate?"

Denburgh checked a control panel. "No!" he reported, shocked. "The pirates have locked us out of the control system!"

"Is there a way to launch it manually?"

"No, there's— Wait!" Denburgh thought a moment. "If we blow the pod's airlock *before* the computer initiates decompression, the pressure of the atmosphere rushing out will be enough to push the pod away. But one of us will have to stay behind—"

Auburn was already pushing Denburgh away. "Yes, yes, yes, just bring here the environmental suits!" She turned back to the away team. "I will remain to launch the pod. Go you with Denburgh."

Deanna felt her stomach twist itself into a knot. "Auburn, we can't just leave you behind!"

The Ichthyan held up her hand. "No arguments! No time! Do as I say!"

Deanna saw the determination in Auburn's eyes. "Aye-aye, sir," she murmured.

Denburgh ran back from the storage locker carrying four sleek environmental suits. Their sheer synthetic fabric was far too flimsy to keep anybody alive in the freezing depths of space. The real protection came from an energy field, or body envelope, that surrounded the wearer. Produced by a mini-generator located in the suit's belt, the body envelope appeared as a thin shimmering yellow halo around the wearer. It would last up to four hours.

"Two minutes, forty seconds to atmospheric evacuation," droned the computer.

As Deanna and the others hurriedly pulled on their suits, Auburn said, "Mr. Denburgh, you will show me how to disable the drive system. Before I die, I wish to keep the Orions from pursuit of you."

Struggling to get the environmental suit on over his bulky work clothes, Denburgh answered, "It's not necessary. The computer will decompress the ship by blowing all the airlocks. The engines aren't designed to survive a temperature drop to absolute zero. They'll explode all by themselves."

"Stupid Orions," Renny said. "They've destroyed themselves, and they don't even know it!"

"They will know it," Auburn stated in a frosty voice. "They will."

"One minute, fifty seconds to shipwide decompression," announced the computer.

Deanna finished sealing up her environmental suit. She fitted the small helmet over her head as Denburgh called out, "Here!" He hastily handed a big, heavy cargo clamp to each of them—except Auburn. "We

have to exit the airlock and use these to attach ourselves to the pod before it launches."

"How will you know when we're ready?" Tronnald
asked Auburn through his helmet.

"I will count to sixty," Auburn said. "You *will* be
ready by then."

Tronnald gulped but didn't argue.

There was no time for good-byes. Denburgh acti-
vated the airlock, and he, Renny, and Tronnald
stepped in. Deanna paused, looking back at Auburn
standing alone in the vast expanse of the pod bay.
"Go, Troi!" Auburn urged, waving impatiently. "Be
not so emotional!"

Be not so emotional? Deanna's mind yelled. But she
said nothing. There was nothing to say. Holding her
cargo clamp so tightly her fingers ached, she whirled
around and ran into the airlock with the others. Then
the door closed, shutting Auburn off alone.

"One minute to shipwide decompression," announced the computer.

With a piercing *whoosh,* the air was sucked out of
the lock. The outer doors parted to reveal the infinity
of open space. Totally black, without perspective,
without guidelines, with only a million twinkling dia-
monds above, below, and stretching forward into all
of eternity—it was like stepping off the edge of time
itself.

Denburgh went first, since he'd space-walked many
times before when doing repair work on the pod's
outer hull. He gently launched himself into nothing-

ness and, grabbing one of the many thin duranium cables that held the cargo pod to the freighter, pulled himself to the pod's hull. The others followed. Deanna, last, stepped into space just as she felt an empathic jolt from Auburn. Not panic, just the animal instinct that responds to danger. *She's alone and terrified*, Deanna thought hopelessly. *Oh, Auburn!*

The pod looked like a giant blister on the freighter's skin, an enormous rounded metal lump about one hundred meters square, attached to one of the freighter's many cargo locks. Normally one would enter it through that lock in the pod bay they'd just left, but the pirates had eliminated that possibility when they code-locked the pod.

Desperate to hold her empathic link to Auburn, yet terrified of the emotions she felt from the Ichthyan, Deanna pulled herself hand over hand along the cable. She located a docking hook on the pod hull and latched on just as the airlock exploded. The atmosphere of the pod bay rushed out, pushing the pod away from its mother ship and out into space. Deanna hung on with all her strength as the pod's limited thrusters kicked in, shooting it farther and farther away. *Auburn!* Deanna called, but she knew it was pointless. She wasn't telepathic, and neither was Auburn.

And then it didn't matter anymore. In a brilliant flash of light, the *Borocco-Kai* exploded, and Auburn was gone.

Space was gone.

Deanna stood in the middle of a bare black room with a precise grid outlined on the walls, ceiling, and floor—Training Holosuite Four. She almost collapsed, but Denburgh grabbed her arm. "Steady there, Cadet," he said jovially.

She looked up at him. "You're . . . you're a real person!"

"The only one in the simulation," Denburgh said. "That's why your empathy worked on me and not the Orions. My name is Lieutenant Commander Hicks. Pleased to meet you."

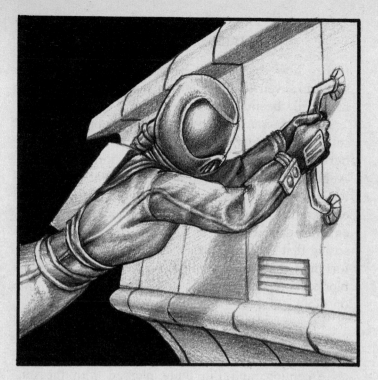

Renny and Tronnald were both staring at Denburgh as well, their eyes wide and a little glassy, as if they'd just survived a war. Which, in a way, they had.

"You may deactivate your environmental suits," came a familiar voice. Deanna turned to see Counselor Gold standing at the holosuite door. "The test is over."

Deanna deactivated her suit and took off the helmet. The only question on her mind was "Did I pass?" but she couldn't say it. She was still in shock from the ending of her simulated adventure. *It was so real!* she thought numbly. *Maybe too real.* It frightened her to realize how easily she'd become wrapped up in the scenario, even to the point of believing that Vandin had really been killed and Auburn really sacrificed.

That, of course, had not really happened. Gold called behind him, "Come in, Cadets," and both Auburn and Vandin entered from the corridor outside. Auburn's face was flushed with triumph as she stepped to Gold's side; obviously she'd found the whole ordeal exhilarating. Vandin, on the other hand, hung back, enveloped in a cloud of despair. The feeling was so strong that Deanna yearned to say something to comfort him, but she knew he would resent it. So she blocked off his emotions and focused her attention on Gold.

"I'd say congratulations, but you all know as well as I do that this test should never have taken place. Not this soon, at any rate. But," said Gold, "I made an exception, and I'm quite pleased with the outcome." He shook hands with Renny, Tronnald, and Deanna. "Cadet Renny, Cadet First-House, Cadet Troi—you three have passed. Your permanent records will reflect your achievement." Then he shook Auburn's hand. "And you will receive special citation for bravery and leadership, Cadet d-ch-Ka."

Deanna felt Auburn's emotions soar higher. *Much higher than this and she'll take off like a balloon,* she thought, smiling at her roommate. Auburn winked back.

Gold turned to Vandin. "I'm sorry, Cadet Sidk." There was genuine regret in the counselor's voice.

Vandin said nothing, just nodded, so Gold addressed them as a group: "Go clean yourselves up, eat a decent meal, and report to my office at sixteen hundred hours for debriefing. Dismissed."

Before Deanna moved, Gold caught her eye. He gave her a quick understanding nod, then exited the holosuite, followed by Hicks.

Deanna didn't know what to do at this point. In order to leave the holosuite, she had to pass Vandin. He seemed glued to one spot, his eyes hollow as he stared out at nothing, stunned by his failure.

When Deanna approached him, however, he rallied his spirits and turned his brilliant grin on her. The sight of that handsome, beaming face made Deanna wonder what Vandin would be like if he wasn't such a cad. Despite his irritating manner, it was hard not to like the flirtatious Xybaki. But more than that, Deanna now felt something she didn't expect—admiration for him. In this moment of defeat, he was trying to be gracious. "Well, so much for the macho method," he said.

"Idiot," Auburn stated flatly. Deanna almost gasped before Auburn added, "I will miss you, Xybaki. You are a good man."

Vandin's emotions spiked, and Deanna was afraid he had taken Auburn's comment the wrong way. But Vandin ua Xadmy Sidk got nose-to-nose with Auburn and murmured softly, though not so softly that the others couldn't hear, "I didn't want to scare you, water woman, but you're really gorgeous, you know

that? I mean, Deanna's drop-dead beautiful, but you—you're *galactic,* know what I mean? I figured if I said so, you'd get all egotistical at me."

Auburn snorted. "As I said—idiot."

"You gave it a good try, Vandin," Renny told him.

"I'm sorry it didn't work out," Tronnald added sincerely.

Vandin shrugged. "Okay, okay, enough. I just want to leave."

"Wait." Deanna draped a chummy arm around Vandin's shoulders. "Let's all go to the mess hall together. We're a team, after all. Right?"

"Right!" the others chorused. Whether he liked it or not, Vandin was swept away for one last dinner on campus.

Deanna felt the Xybaki's insatiable ego eat up the attention, and she smiled.

CHAPTER

12

San Francisco
Earth

Deanna wished she could smile as she walked briskly along Franklin Avenue. The beautiful city of San Francisco, its sky a brilliant blue and its streets bustling with activity, did not lift her spirits. All she could think about was her mother.

Counselor Gold had given Deanna permission to leave campus, a rare privilege. Too bad she had to use that privilege for this purpose. *This should be a joyous visit,* she thought in despair. *You should want to do this.* But Deanna wished she were doing anything *but* this.

The elaborately carved oak door of a grand Victorian mansion swung open at Deanna's approach.

Little One! came a familiar mental voice from inside.

Deanna climbed the steps leading up to the porch. She nodded to Xelo, who had opened the door, then turned to her mother, who waited, smiling, just beyond the entrance. "You're not angry with me anymore, Mother?"

Lwaxana gestured to herself with a "Who, little ol' me?" expression. *Angry? Why should I be angry? You passed that* Borocco-Kai *whatchamajig, didn't you?* She ushered Deanna inside, and Xelo dutifully closed the door. *I'm simply happy that you've come, Little One! It took you long enough.*

Deanna wanted to explain why she was here, but the sight of the mansion's foyer stopped her dead in her tracks. "Mother . . . you *live* here?" Deanna gasped, staring at the fine wood-carved interior, the lush draperies, the huge crystal chandelier—everything, no doubt, authentic decor from Earth's Victorian era.

Lwaxana brushed off her daughter's awe. *Oh, these are temporary quarters,* she projected. *Nothing special.*

"Nothing special?" Deanna practically reeled from the sheer luxury of the place. "Mother, when in the world are you going to be honest with me?"

Lwaxana ignored the question. *Come, let's sit in the parlor. That was the custom in these old houses. It's quite enchanting, really.* She led the way into a small room, and mother and daughter sat on the plush couch.

Deanna started to talk, but Lwaxana put a finger on her lips. *Let me speak first.* Quickly she added, "Out loud, all right?" She thought for a moment. "I'm proud of you, Deanna. I sensed your success the moment the test ended. But the fact remains that you did a very foolish thing."

"No, Mother," Deanna cut in, "I did what I had to do. More than that, I did what I wanted to do. That's the real issue here, isn't it?" She paused. "Look, I know you had plans for me on Betazed. I know you hoped I would follow certain paths that you felt were the best for me. But I've discovered my own path. Let me follow it."

"Whatever makes you think I'm not? I let you apply to Starfleet, didn't I?"

"Yes, but since then you've done everything in your power to persuade me to change my mind. Tell me something—why did you come here?"

Lwaxana looked exasperated. "You keep asking me that question when the answer is obvious: I got a job."

"No, Mother." Deanna stared straight into Lwaxana's eyes, looking for something in their depths. She knew she was hitting close to home when she felt a hint of guilt leak through her mother's shields. "Tell me the truth. You've got to say it out loud or you'll never accept it."

Lwaxana broke eye contact and quickly rose to her feet. "I can't imagine what you're talking about."

Walking over to a table, she began rearranging roses in a gold vase. She seemed unusually absorbed in the task.

"Do you know what the funniest part of this whole thing is?" Deanna said casually. "I've finally decided what to specialize in at the Academy. You'll never guess who helped me make the choice. You."

Lwaxana turned. "Me?"

"Don't you see? It was because of all our arguing that I took the *Borocco-Kai* test in the first place. I thought that no matter how horrible it was, I would show you that I could handle it. But you know what?" She shrugged, amazed at herself. "I kind of enjoyed it. I mean, it was difficult, but it was the most exciting experience I've ever had. I helped my team beat the scenario. And," she added, "I think I helped a few people along the way."

"Well," said Lwaxana, scrutinizing her new rose arrangement, "your Starfleet career is off to a blazing start. That's what you wanted, isn't it?"

"Yes, but I want *you* to be happy, too. Mother, our relationship can't go on like this. Be honest with me, please. *Why did you come here?*"

It started small, just a hint of emotion, a mere drop that leaked through shields much stronger than Deanna's own. And then Deanna was hit by a great wave of grief as those shields broke down. Strangely enough, the assault of her mother's emotions didn't hurt. Deanna's own shields held firm, and she knew without a doubt that her own power held them there.

Lwaxana's eyes brimmed with tears as she confessed, "Oh, Little One, I don't want to lose you. If something happened to you out there . . . well, when your father died, you were the one who pulled me through. Don't you realize that? I miss him so much . . . but with you at my side, I never feel lonely. You're all I have left." She gave a helpless little shrug, unable to say more.

Deanna reached out for her mother. "Thank you," she whispered.

Lwaxana held her tight. "No, thank *you*, Little One. I suppose I knew I'd have to admit the truth sooner or later." She gently pulled away, sniffling. "I'll quit my teaching post at the Academy tomorrow, all right?"

"Are you sure—"

"Yes, I'm sure. If I'm going to be honest, I might as well go all the way." Taking a deep breath, she plunged on, "I contracted for the post just so I could be near you. Oh, that's absolutely ludicrous, I admit, but . . . I missed you too much." She plopped down on the couch, looking for all the world like a bored child. "Besides, teaching is infernally dull!"

Deanna laughed. "You were good at it, though."

"Good? I was excellent. I was exceptional!" Lwaxana pondered a moment. "Hmm . . . maybe if I picked a more interesting subject I could—"

"Don't you dare," Deanna warned.

"And why not, Miss Selfish? Maybe I'm simply not cut out for xenosociology."

"No, Mother!"

"But think of it—mother and daughter, out there among the stars—"

"No, Mother!"

Lwaxana threw her hands in the air, a graceful gesture that somehow still came across as comical. "Well, that's it, then. I'm beaten! But you say I did help you choose your specialty at the Academy?"

Deanna felt her cheeks flush. "All right, I suppose it's my turn to make a confession. Here it is: You've been right all along, Mother."

"Of course I have!" Lwaxana blinked. "About what?"

Deanna chuckled. "About all the advice you've given me over the years. No matter what I ever tried to do, you had some opinion about it. I used to hate that, but now I understand what you were trying to do." Deanna grew serious. "Everybody, including me, needs advice. I accept that now. But knowing when to give advice and how to give it has been the problem between us all along. I want to help people, as you've helped me, Mother, but I want to be sure the people I advise really want my advice. I've recently heard about the new Galaxy-class starships that are being built at the fleet yards on Mars. They say those ships will be the first to have full-time counselors on board. I want to be one of those counselors."

A moment passed before Lwaxana responded to this announcement. "You won't consider a nice safe desk job at Starfleet Headquarters, hm?"

Deanna shook her head. "Nope."

Lwaxana sighed. "Oh, very well. Mr. Xelo will just have to keep me up to date on your whereabouts as you flit from one end of the galaxy to the other."

Deanna wasn't sure if sailing through space in a ship the size of a small nation could be considered *flitting*, but she took her mother's words as a sign of acceptance.

"Ship's Counselor Deanna Troi," she said, feeling the words on her tongue, smooth as Thalian chocolate. "Ship's Counselor Deanna Troi." She smiled.

It had a nice ring to it.

About the Authors

Delivered one Christmas morning by reindeer instead of a stork, Bobbi JG Weiss has spent most of her life avoiding reality and to this day still keeps up a personal correspondence with Rudolph. Clinging to the belief that cartoons are real, that cats speak English, and that coffee bestows superpowers, she is fit for no profession other than that of writer. With her husband she has penned novels, comic books, animation, trading cards, CD-ROMs and dumb little comic strips for orange juice cartons. One day she hopes to *become* a cartoon.

Stolen from Gypsies as a child, David Cody Weiss was raised in suburban comfort until his teens. Then his true heritage claimed him and he broke loose of the middle class straitjacket, going forth and having many jobs (no two alike!). When he acquired a wife (and partner), he decided that becoming a writer was better than working for a living. His goal is to become independently wealthy, and he thanks you for buying this book.

Pocket Books presents a new, illustrated series for younger readers based on the hit television show:

Young Jake Sisko is looking for friends aboard the space station. He finds Nog, a Ferengi his own age, and together they find a whole lot of trouble!

Published by Pocket Books

954-08

STAR TREK®

STARFLEET ACADEMY®

The first adventures of cadets James T. Kirk, Leonard McCoy and the Vulcan Spock!

From Spock's momentous decision to attend Starfleet Academy on Earth, through his first meeting with the medical student McCoy and their action-packed adventure with the ultra-serious, ultra-daring Cadet Kirk, these adventures will take readers "where no one has gone before"™—back to the very beginning!

1 CRISIS ON VULCAN 00078-0/$3.99
By Brad and Barbara Strickland

2 AFTERSHOCK 00079-9/$3.99
By John Vornholt

3 CADET KIRK 00077-2/$3.99
By Diane Carey

A MINSTREL® BOOK
Published by Pocket Books

Simon & Schuster Mail Order Dept. BWB
200 Old Tappan Rd., Old Tappan, N.J. 07675

Please send me the books I have checked above. I am enclosing $_____ (please add $0.75 to cover the postage and handling for each order. Please add appropriate sales tax). Send check or money order--no cash or C.O.D.'s please. Allow up to six weeks for delivery. For purchase over $10.00 you may use VISA: card number, expiration date and customer signature must be included.

Name _____

Address _____

City _____ State/Zip _____

VISA Card # _____ Exp.Date _____

Signature _____ 1210-01